TARGET ONE

(THE SPY GAME—BOOK 1)

JACK MARS

Jack Mars

Jack Mars is the USA Today bestselling author of the LUKE STONE thriller series, which includes seven books. He is also the author of the new FORGING OF LUKE STONE prequel series, comprising six books; of the AGENT ZERO spy thriller series, comprising twelve books; of the TROY STARK thriller series, comprising three books; and of the SPY GAME thriller series, comprising three books.

Jack loves to hear from you, so please feel free to visit www.Jackmarsauthor.com to join the email list, receive a free book, receive free giveaways, connect on Facebook and Twitter, and stay in touch!

ISBN: 978-1-0943-7761-2

BOOKS BY JACK MARS

THE SPY GAME
TARGET ONE (Book #1)
TARGET TWO (Book #2)
TARGET THREE (Book #3)

TROY STARK THRILLER SERIES
ROGUE FORCE (Book #1)
ROGUE COMMAND (Book #2)
ROGUE TARGET (Book #3)

LUKE STONE THRILLER SERIES
ANY MEANS NECESSARY (Book #1)
OATH OF OFFICE (Book #2)
SITUATION ROOM (Book #3)
OPPOSE ANY FOE (Book #4)
PRESIDENT ELECT (Book #5)
OUR SACRED HONOR (Book #6)
HOUSE DIVIDED (Book #7)

FORGING OF LUKE STONE PREQUEL SERIES
PRIMARY TARGET (Book #1)
PRIMARY COMMAND (Book #2)
PRIMARY THREAT (Book #3)
PRIMARY GLORY (Book #4)
PRIMARY VALOR (Book #5)
PRIMARY DUTY (Book #6)

AN AGENT ZERO SPY THRILLER SERIES
AGENT ZERO (Book #1)
TARGET ZERO (Book #2)
HUNTING ZERO (Book #3)
TRAPPING ZERO (Book #4)
FILE ZERO (Book #5)
RECALL ZERO (Book #6)
ASSASSIN ZERO (Book #7)
DECOY ZERO (Book #8)
CHASING ZERO (Book #9)

VENGEANCE ZERO (Book #10)
ZERO ZERO (Book #11)
ABSOLUTE ZERO (Book #12)

PROLOGUE

He stared at the building in the darkness, looming before him, and rubbed his hand slowly on the cold handle of his gun. Glancing around to make sure no one was in sight, he approached, one foot before the other, creeping up along the back wall, keeping in the deep shadows of the oak trees lining the edge of the lawn. No streetlight penetrated here. Someone could walk by on the sidewalk just ten yards away and not see him.

The time had come.

A lone guard stood fifty feet away, guarding the one entrance he needed. The assassin smiled to himself. The man had no idea he was about to lose his life.

He approached the guard with infinite care, drawing the gun from its holster without a sound.

The guard was facing away, looking at something on the upper floor. He remained oblivious to the assassin and started humming a popular tune to himself.

The assassin got to within five feet of the man and took aim. He would shoot him in the back of the head—that way, he would never know what hit him.

Just then, a twig snapped under his foot.

The guard spun, hand going to his gun, eyes searching the darkness for the intruder.

He never got a chance to spot him. The assassin shot him in the head, the usual crack of the shot deadened by a compact, top-of-the-line silencer. The bullet excavated a trough of flesh and bone, and the guard dropped to the ground, dead.

The assassin rolled the body behind a bush, gave a quick glance around to make sure no one else was in sight, then darted to the entrance and tried the handle. Locked.

He holstered his gun, pulled out a set of lockpicks, and had the door open in less than a minute.

The alarm went off, its electronic blare echoing through the darkened halls of the museum. He knew it would. He also knew that he had 180 seconds to clear the place.

The room beyond felt like a cavern, a cold, humid draft wafting through it, the soaring walls lined with bas-reliefs, statues, and large glass cases filled with ancient relics.

But there was only one relic that interested him.

He hurried up the marble stairs to the second floor, taking them three at a time, counting the remaining seconds in his head, the alarm shrieking. While his expertise lay with targeted killings, in the course of his career he had learned a great deal about breaking and entering. It was often part of his job, and it was that skillset that got him hired for this particular mission. Being a heartless killing machine came as a bonus.

He turned right and sprinted down the hall, not stopping to read the sign. He had memorized the layout by heart and knew he was entering the Egyptian wing.

Upon entering, he stopped in his tracks, staring at what he had come to steal.

The ancient Canopic jar.

It was one of a set of five, all made of gleaming alabaster and in perfect condition, untouched by the millennia. Canopic jars contained the internal organs of an Egyptian mummy, and were buried with it to rejoin the body in the afterlife. The number of jars marked this set as unusual. Every other set numbered only four, each adorned with one of the heads of the four sons of Horus. He hadn't known this until he got this assignment. It always paid to do your research. One jar had a lid in the shape of a baboon's head, symbolizing the god Hapi, who guarded the lungs. Duamutef with the jackal's head guarded the stomach. The human-headed god Imsety guarded the liver. Qebehsenuef, the falcon-headed god, guarded the intestines.

Then there was the fifth, with a lion's head on the lid representing the goddess Sekhmet, guarding … what?

It wasn't his job to know.

The alarm continued shrieking. He'd have to get out fast.

He aimed at the top of the cabinet, well away from the jar, and fired.

The bullet went straight through the glass and shattered it into a thousand pieces.

He winced as the sound of a second alarm reverberated around him, overlapping the first.

Grabbing the lion-headed jar, he found it heavier than expected. Fifty pounds at least. Whatever lay inside, it sure as hell wasn't someone's internal organs.

He set his curiosity aside. It wasn't his job to know. It was his job to procure it for his bosses. And whatever it was, it was valuable enough to hire someone like him to get it, and then keep him on retainer. Why keep him after he'd done the job? He didn't know that either.

The assassin turned and sprinted out of the room as fast as he could, slid as he turned the corner, and pelted down the steps.

For a minute he thought he'd gotten away, that he was going to make it.

He was wrong.

A bullet moaned past his head to take out a chunk of marble on the bannister beside him.

He glanced back to see another guard at the top of the stairs, gun raised as he took careful aim.

This was not according to plan. There was only supposed to be one guard. His employers had given him faulty intel.

Forty-five seconds until the cops arrived. He had a quick decision to make.

Run for it and risk a bullet in his head, or fight back and risk the cops.

The second shot, cracking off the stair at his feet, made the decision for him.

He set the jar on a step, steadying it with one hand, and raised his gun.

No fear. That guard was a simple paid employee facing one of the world's finest assassins, who got paid more than the museum staff would earn in one hundred lifetimes.

A single, perfect shot, square in the guard's forehead.

The man collapsed.

Twenty seconds.

Out the open door and into the frozen Boston night, onto the waiting motorcycle, and down the back alley.

Ten seconds.

Police sirens wailed behind him, already distant, pulling up to a museum he had left.

He grinned as he merged onto I-95.

The jar was his.

And the world was about to change forever.

That was what his employer had said. Those were the exact words he had used.

"The world is about to change forever."

CHAPTER ONE

The fist slammed into Jacob Snow's face, making his head snap hard to the right. The chair he was tied to rocked back and forth, and only Jacob's widespread legs kept him from toppling over.

He didn't want to fall to the floor, because then they might start kicking him.

"Tell us who you work for," the man who had punched him demanded, his words heavy with an Arabic accent.

He spoke in English, because he didn't know Jacob spoke Arabic.

Jacob said nothing in either language, or any of the several others he spoke.

The fist slammed into his face again. One of Jacob's eyes had almost swollen shut, at least two of his teeth were loose, and his mouth filled with the coppery tang of fresh blood.

"Tell us what we want to know and the beatings will stop," another of the Arabs said.

There were three of them, members of The Sword of the Righteous, a splinter group of Al Qaeda targeting foreign aid workers. They had captured him in the suburbs of Damascus, bundled him into the trunk of a car, and dragged him to this cellar.

Now they wanted to know why he had been sneaking around their secret headquarters, the location of which was supposedly a secret even to most members of The Sword of the Righteous.

Another fist, to the stomach this time. Jacob coughed and bent over as much as his bonds would allow. The punch to the stomach was followed by a vicious uppercut that felt like it nearly decapitated him.

The real thing would probably come later. These people liked cutting off the heads of Westerners working for the Red Cross or Save the Children and displaying them around town.

Especially in front of schools. They called it "spiritual education." That's how these guys rolled.

The man beating him took a step back, shaking out his hand. Jacob could see all the knuckles were scuffed and bleeding, a small compensation for being turned into a human punching bag. The three terrorists moved away to the far end of the bare cellar and got into a huddle.

"This man doesn't break," the one who had been punching him said, speaking in Arabic and presuming Jacob couldn't understand.

"Let's cut his balls off. He'll speak then."

"No, he won't," said the youngest. "He won't have anything left to lose."

"A finger, then. Let me cut off a finger."

"Oh, Ahmed," the youngest said with a sigh. "You are always in a hurry to cut people. Let's beat him more."

"And you have a weak stomach," Ahmed snapped. "We've been beating him for an hour. It's not working."

"Maybe electrocute him?"

"That might work."

"I still say we should cut him."

While the three terrorists talked, Jacob let out a slow breath, forcing his aching muscles to relax. A feeling of warmth passed through him. Calm.

And then, as he had learned from his parents as a child, he took a deep breath and slowly let it out, forcing his muscles to relax. With a special maneuver, he dislocated one shoulder, suppressing the urge to scream as pain lanced down the entire limb. He pulled his arm out of its bonds, and popped the arm back into place. Relief flooded him as the throbbing pain began to ebb. Then he did the same with the other arm.

Some kids dreamed of running away and joining the circus. Jacob didn't have to. He grew up in the circus.

Now free, he stood up and grabbed the chair.

The terrorists whirled around, mouths agape.

Too late. Jacob Snow was already charging, the chair upraised like a club.

He brought it down on the first terrorist's head with a crunch. The man sagged to the floor, unconscious.

The other two backpedaled and drew their guns, but before they could aim, Jacob hurled the chair at them. It struck one of the terrorists in the stomach, sending him staggering backwards to bump into the third. That screwed up his aim and his shot went wide. The next instant, he caught Jacob's fist in his jaw.

The blow laid him flat, as unconscious as the man he had hit over the head with the chair.

The second terrorist, the one hit in the midriff, got his balance and raised his weapon. Jacob tackled him.

They rolled over and over, the terrorist struggling to keep the gun. Jacob grabbed his wrist and twisted it.

A satisfying snap and the pistol fell out of the terrorist's hand.

Straddling him, he gave the terrorist three quick punches to the throat, collapsing his windpipe. The man bucked and gasped underneath him. Jacob stood, leaving him to choke to death.

Jacob let out a gust of air and picked up one of the pistols. A Russian-made GSh-18 with a long box magazine carrying 18 9×19mm Parabellum rounds. Standard issue for the Syrian Army and Police Forces.

It could have come from either. Fighters for The Sword of the Righteous killed members of both forces almost as eagerly as they killed foreigners trying to help sick children and injured civilians. Jacob tucked the pistol into the waistline of his jeans and grabbed an AK-47 leaning against the wall.

All three men were down for the count. No, not quite. One groaned and shifted his leg a little. He was waking up. One of the others would wake up soon, too.

Jacob closed his eyes for a moment, but that didn't hide the ugly reality facing him. He knew what he needed to do.

Jacob didn't like killing helpless people. He preferred a fair fight, but he was deep in enemy territory and he didn't know how many more terrorists might be around.

He didn't have time to tie them up, not when more of them might come downstairs at any moment. And even if he did have time, their friends would release them and they'd go on to kill more innocent people. Or send out his description through the Dark Web for any Islamist out there to hunt him down and kill him. People like this had to be stopped, or they'd up their relentless body count of the innocent.

It became a math problem, a horrible summing up of how to let as few helpless people die as possible. Killing them was the only right answer.

All that was true, but deep down Jacob knew it was all an excuse. It really came down to them or him, and when it came down to that decision, Jacob Snow always chose himself.

But he couldn't risk a shot. Who knew what kind of neighbors these scumbags had?

He spotted a sheathed knife on the belt of one of the terrorists, the same one who had been so eager to cut off Jacob's body parts.

Jacob stepped over to him.

The knife came free from the sheath with a soft hiss. Jacob held it in his hand and stared at it in the cold light of the bare bulb hanging from the concrete ceiling. Then he turned back to the men on the ground. He knew what he had to do.

As he knelt by the man closest to him, Jacob whispered, "I'm sorry," then he leaned in and placed the knife's keen edge along the man's neck …

… and then paused, bile rising up in his throat.

The image of a young Pathan warrior, lying helpless on the floor of a cave, flashed through his mind. His throat had opened up so easily, blood spouting out like a burst water balloon.

Never again.

Jacob pulled back, his brow shiny with sweat.

The Arab groaned, shifting a second time.

Jacob turned the knife around and smacked him on the skull with the metal pommel, knocking him out cold.

Then Jacob moved onto the next man, the man whose throat he collapsed. Best to make sure. No, he was dead. Killed in an open fight. Jacob felt nothing for him.

He knelt down beside the third man and leaned in close to him. This one had hung back a bit during the torture, reluctant to take part. He'd been the one who had saved the most important part of Jacob's anatomy. Too bad. In another world, if this Syrian had grown up differently, he and Jacob could have been friends.

"Goodbye," he said. Then he smacked him over the head with the pommel.

This is a mistake. You're allowing murderers to go free, to kill again.

Killing them is the logical thing to do. Killing them is the right *thing to do.*

NO.

Jacob stood, lost his balance for a moment, and steadied himself. Again he closed his eyes. He counted to three, a mental trick to switch from one feeling to another. He could fell regret and self-disgust later. Right now he had to get out of here. Right now he had to finish the mission.

Jacob opened his eyes and hurried up the concrete steps, unbolted the heavy steel door and, AK-47 at the ready, rushed into the ground floor of the terrorist safe house. He needed to kill anyone else in it and get the hell out as fast as possible.

The ground floor was a typical Syrian home. A few sparsely decorated rooms with thick carpeting and low tables and no chairs.

Jacob moved cautiously, at pains not to make a sound. Then he heard a clatter of metal from the kitchen. Someone was at home.

He slowly stepped into the kitchen doorway, the AK-47 to his shoulder, and quickly spotted the terrorist. The guy, who wore a red and white checkered kaffiyeh around his head, sprinted through a doorway into the kitchen, wheeling his arm as he ran, like a baseball player rounding the base.

Jacob spotted the grenade in his hand. That's what he hated about fighting terrorists. The idiots didn't care about their own lives and would do crazy moves like throwing a grenade indoors at point blank range.

No time for stealth. Jacob's AK-47 cracked, and the terrorist jerked as the bullet hit him in the chest. The guy ran three more steps and then fell almost at Jacob's feet. The grenade bounced off the floor and rolled into a corner.

Jacob raced back into the living room and smashed through the glass of the front window. He landed in a roll and ran for the front gate. Like most residences in the country, it was surrounded by a concrete wall with a metal gate. Given the state of their nation, home security was a prime concern for Syrians. The grenade detonated when he was halfway there, pushing a blast front out the window and alerting the whole damn neighborhood.

Great, Jacob thought. *That's just freaking great.*

Having no time to fiddle with the gate lock, he slung his AK-47 and threw himself at the ten-foot concrete wall. His fingers barely grasped the top lip of the wall as the front of his foot pushed up against the wall's face, propelling him up in a move every raw recruit learns in basic training.

Mom and Dad had taught him that trick when he was five.

Just then, the crack of an AK behind him told him he hadn't entirely cleared the house. A bullet gouged a dent into the concrete wall inches to his right. Jacob vaulted over the wall, cutting a hand on the broken glass set all along the top, and landed with a roll on the street outside.

Jacob unslung his AK as a taxi came around the corner. In his peripheral vision, he saw a couple of people scatter and a door slam shut. No one would help him. He was used to that.

The taxi screeched to a stop as Jacob stepped into the middle of the road and leveled his weapon.

"I need you to take me to—"

"No! No!" the taxi driver leapt out of his vehicle and fled.

"Fine," Jacob said, hopping into the driver's seat. "I'll drive myself."

Jacob peeled out down the road, the terrorist in the upper window of the safe house firing after him. Jacob shoved a twenty-dollar bill into the glove compartment for the driver to find later. Everyone here wanted hard currency, not the almost worthless Syrian pound.

As he turned the far corner, the terrorist's last shot took out the taxi's back window. Jacob cursed and added a hundred-dollar bill to the twenty.

Within minutes, he was back at the CIA safe house, giving a full report. The airstrike would take out the headquarters that night.

But that was no victory, only round one, because what he had learned in his surveillance of the headquarters, the information he had nearly given his life for, was that The Sword of the Righteous was far, far bigger than anyone had realized.

Using state-of-the-art electronic surveillance, he had been able to view the computer screens of those working inside, as well as monitor all their phone calls, and he had learned that this wasn't their only headquarters. They had branches in Tripoli, Benghazi, Port Suez, Cairo, Beirut, Baghdad, and Basra.

Probably more, because he had only been able to scan for half an hour before he got nabbed.

Half an hour. In only half an hour he'd overheard them speaking on equal terms with several other branches. Not issuing orders like a central command would have done, but trading information and discussing strategy.

He wasn't cutting the head off the organization, because it was a hydra, with a dozen heads that would grow back twofold when you cut off one.

The fight was just beginning.

CHAPTER TWO

Two days later . . .

Jacob Snow stood in the CIA office in Athens doing his debriefing, his face still puffy from the beating he had taken two days before, one hand swathed in gauze from the cut he got climbing over the broken glass on top of the wall. And he had bled all over that poor man's taxi. At least his teeth hadn't fallen out.

He'd worried about that. Jacob cared about his appearance. Bruises came and went, but an attractive smile could seduce from a hundred yards.

Not that station director Tyler Wallace cared about his smile. The hulking African-American ex-Marine preferred scowling, and he sure was scowling now.

Not at Jacob, but at what he had called him in for.

"You've done a good job, as usual, Jacob. That intel is going to lead to a dozen airstrikes like the one we just did in Damascus."

"It won't help. By the time you've pinpointed all those different headquarters, they'll have evacuated. You shouldn't have hit the Damascus branch until you knew about the others."

Wallace's frowned deepened. "I know that. You think I'm an idiot?"

"No, but the higher-ups are."

"The president needed something solid for the midterms."

"The president should take the long view."

"Fat chance. Now on to new business. We've gotten some strange intel through our operatives in Cairo," he said, "and we think it's linked to a robbery in Boston."

"What kind of intel?" Jacob asked.

"From an undercover agent in The Sword of the Righteous. The Cairo branch. He's not in too deep, so a lot of his information is secondhand, and none of it is confirmed, but it's troubling enough."

"It's always troubling with that crowd," Jacob grumbled, unconsciously rubbing the biggest bruise, one that made one of his high cheekbones stand out like a plum.

"You look fine," Wallace said with a dismissive wave of his hand. "My God, I've never met a man who cared so much about his looks."

"It's handy when trying to get into people's confidence."

"Is that a double entendre?" Wallace grunted. "If you care about your precious face so much, maybe you should stop getting beaten up by terrorists."

"That's your fault, not mine," Jacob said with a smile.

"Whatever. Our mole in The Sword of the Righteous says they're planning on hitting our embassy in Cairo, but first they need something from Boston. And just a couple of days ago, someone stole an Egyptian artifact from a museum in Boston."

"That's a pretty thin connection."

"It's gets better, or worse. The Sword of the Righteous is trying to get the relic from a Boston crime boss, an Iraqi named Omar Al-Fulan. They're paying him in heroin."

"Why would they need an ancient Egyptian relic to attack the U.S. embassy? That makes no sense."

"No, it doesn't, but our operative is sure there's a connection. Maybe they want to sell it and buy some special weapon?"

"Why not just sell the heroin and do that?"

Wallace shrugged. "Maybe they think they can get more for the artifact. Or maybe it's the artifact itself somehow. It's unique."

"What is it, anyway?"

"A Canopic jar. When someone got mummified, they put their organs into four different jars, except this was from a burial that had five Canopic jars. The fifth had a totally different design than anything ever seen before. It's all in the report."

Wallace pushed a black folder across his table, sealed with a gold stamp.

Jacob glanced at the folder but didn't pick it up. "What do we know about Omar al-Fulan?"

"Not much. He's forty-two, mixed Iraqi-Egyptian heritage, comes from a prominent family of merchants. There are rumors he's involved in the drug trade, but there's never been enough evidence to bring charges, and trust me, the DEA has tried. The guy is also a bit of a playboy, a habitual gambler. He can be ruthless and he's not above using violence. Once again, not enough evidence. He's not known to be affiliated with any terrorist groups."

"Strictly in it for the money, eh?"

"Yeah. Now the Canopic jar was discovered by an American archaeologist who found it on a dig in Egypt a couple of years ago.

She's running an excavation in Morocco right now, and we think she might end up a target. Even if she doesn't, she might have some insight into why this Canopic jar is so special. So I want you to run through the file and pick one of our Moroccan operatives to contact her."

Jacob cocked his head. "Pick one of the Moroccan operatives? You mean you don't want me to go myself?"

Wallace grimaced. "Look in the mirror, Jacob. You're a mess."

"I think I can manage a flight to Morocco and a chat with some archaeologist."

"You've been in Syria for the past month," the station chief said. "And the month before that, you were in Lebanon. And the month before that, you were in Iraq."

"You wanted me to get rid of that Sunni arms running operation and I did. Then you wanted me to eavesdrop on a terrorist nest in Damascus and I did. You can't really complain."

"My point is that you've been on the front line for far too long."

"So Morocco will be like a vacation," Jacob said with a smile. He shouldn't have smiled. That made his fat lip crack open again.

"Yeah, right. Not with your luck. Look, Jacob. We go way back. Let me tell you not as your boss, but as a friend. You've been driving yourself too hard. You need a break."

"Fine. After I talk to this archaeologist chick, I'll lounge on the beach near Essaouira for a week or two. Do some kite surfing. Happy?"

"I'll be happy when we've wiped out The Sword of the Righteous."

"You're going to have a long wait for happiness then," Jacob said, picking up the folder and breaking the seal, an act that, for anyone under his level of security clearance, would have earned them ten years in Guantanamo.

"Who is this archaeologist, anyway?" he asked as he pulled out the dossier.

"Dr. Jana Peters."

Jacob nearly dropped the folder. Wallace must have caught his expression because he asked, "You know her?"

"Yeah," Jacob mumbled. "I know her."

Or know of her, at least. I wanted to keep it that way.

Suddenly Jacob regretted being so quick to volunteer to do this mission himself.

His boss's eyes narrowed. "Is this going to be a problem?"

"No."

No more of a problem than being captured by terrorists.

Maybe he could convince Wallace to send him back to Syria instead.

CHAPTER THREE

A field near Asilah, northwestern Morocco

Dr. Jana Peters wiped her brow and clambered out of the trench she and her team had excavated. There was a common saying that Morocco was a cold country with a hot sun. Being noon, all she was feeling right now was a blasting heat from the searing ball of flame in a pale blue sky. The Moroccan sun ignored the fact that it was winter. But as soon as that sun set, the temperature would plunge and she and her team would have to put on sweaters to keep from shivering in their tents.

They sure weren't shivering now. She looked out over the small excavation. A dozen young men and women labored away, a mixture of graduate students and younger undergraduates, along with a couple of local workers she had hired when she had arrived two weeks ago.

A survey done in the 1990s had identified this area as the site of a possible Roman villa. It had only been a surface survey, a simple technique in which archaeologists got into a line with each person a couple of yards apart, and then walked slowly along the field looking for artifacts.

While the bulk of any ancient site remained locked underground, buried under centuries of accumulation of soil, some artifacts always made it to the surface thanks to burrowing animals and the action of farmers' ploughs.

The survey had found a couple of Roman coins from the second century AD, a *terra sigillata* lamp from the same period, and several colorful tesserae, little squares of colored stone that make up a mosaic.

On the first week of the excavation, Jana's team had cleared the site of underbrush and dug a test trench in the most promising area.

That had uncovered the corner of a mosaic, a large and elaborate floor decoration consisting of thousands of small colored stones arranged into figures or scenes. Mosaics were common in wealthy Roman homes and public buildings, although the artistry of this one set it apart.

While the portion of mosaic her students had found measured only a couple of yards across and punctured by not one but two holes burrowed by rodents, it was clearly a Roman work from the second century AD.

The design reminded her of one she had seen once in the Museo Arqueológico Nacional in Madrid. The edge showed one panel and part of the other, each with its own picture. One showed a bull, expertly executed with different shades of brown and black tesserae to create shading, and the portion of the other had a young man in a tunic.

Beneath the portion still covered by soil would be a second, identical man. Taurus and Gemini. Two of the constellations of the zodiac. The rest of the mosaic would have the other ten signs around its edge, and some central decoration they had yet to reveal.

Dr. Jana Peters took a deep breath and smiled. Not only had they found a piece of ancient art *in situ*, they had found the foundation walls of several of the villa's rooms and numerous artifacts. It would be easy to get funding to excavate the rest of the site.

Movement out of the corner of her eye caught her attention. She turned and saw half a dozen burly locals heading their direction, carrying shovels, picks, and trowels. They were led by a thin, older Moroccan in a suit.

Some of the undergraduates stopped their work to stare. Jana glanced at them and they got back to it.

Jana turned to the newcomers as they walked up.

"Good morning," the man in the suit said in English.

"Sabah alkhayr," Jana replied in Arabic.

The man smiled and continued in Arabic. "I have heard you speak Arabic, Dr. Peters. Allow me to introduce myself. I am Professor Mallam Alaoui of the Abdelmalek Essaâdi University in Tangier. I teach archaeology and have conducted several excavations throughout the country."

"I've heard of you, professor," she said, shaking his hand. "I've never had the pleasure of meeting you."

The professor grimaced. "I wish we could meet under better circumstances. I am afraid that I am a little embarrassed by this, but I have been instructed by the government to take over the excavation."

"Take over the excavation?" Jana exclaimed. "Why?"

"I am afraid the government has decided that this area is just too important to leave in the hands of foreigners. I apologize. That is very rude of them, not to mention inhospitable and ungrateful. Your excavations in this country have enriched our national heritage. A significant find of this nature will have a very positive effect on Morocco's tourism, and that in turn will have a very positive effect on

16

the economy. The national government thinks it would reflect better on Morocco if it was excavated by Moroccans."

Jana gestured at the workers, all of whom had stopped now. "We have Moroccans on our team, including our foreman and one of the graduate students."

"That's true and I appreciate that, but I am sure you can appreciate that an important site such as this should be investigated and managed by a Moroccan. We had hoped that you would be willing to step aside and let us do this, since you have already done so much of the preliminary work."

"I don't think so," Jana replied.

"This is a very important find," Dr. Alaoui said, "and I am sorry to take it from you, but my instructions from the government are quite clear."

"I need to see documentation for this," she said, her anger rising.

"Of course." Dr. Alaoui reached inside his jacket and pulled out a sheaf of papers.

He handed over a document in Arabic, stamped and signed by the Minister of Culture and Antiquities. Jana looked at the date. Yesterday.

They could have at least called first, Jana thought. Although considering how Moroccan bureaucracy worked, she wasn't surprised.

Something niggled at the back of her mind, though. It took her a moment to put her finger on it.

"These documents look all in order," she admitted, "but I'm surprised they put you on this dig. You specialize in the prehistoric period, don't you?"

The Moroccan archaeologist nodded. "I do, but no one else was available."

"Oh! But you did that excavation of the temple of Hadrian near Rabat, didn't you?"

"True. So I have a little experience in Roman sites."

Jana's face hardened. "Except there's no temple of Hadrian near Rabat. And the real Professor Alaoui sure didn't run it."

The Moroccan's face darkened. "What are you implying?"

Jana waved the papers in his face and switched to English so the bulk of her team could follow the conversation. The Moroccan members were already paying rapt attention.

"You aren't who you say you are, and these papers are fake. I just remembered that the minister couldn't have signed these papers yesterday as the date implies, because the day before yesterday he left for a conference in Tunisia. And he's still there."

"They're antiquities thieves!" one of the graduate students shouted. "They heard about the mosaic and they want to steal it."

"You just earned an A," Jana said, tearing up the fake papers. She tossed the shreds into the fake professor's face. "And you earned an F."

"Get out of here!" the Moroccan bellowed. His men edged forward. Jana's own people jumped out of the trench to face them.

"Leave, or I'll call the police," Jana said.

"Move!" The fake Professor Mallam Alaoui tried to shove her aside, and then did the worst thing he could have done.

He copped a feel.

Not the worst thing he could have done to her. The worst thing he could have done to himself.

Because the next thing he felt after the firm curve of her ass was the hard impact of her elbow on his face while at the same time her leg swept the back of his own.

He stumbled back and fell. The Moroccans cried out, outraged and shocked. Jana howled in rage as the fake professor's men converged on her. She ducked a swing that would have knocked her out cold and flipped her attacker so he landed hard on his back. The others surged forward, intent on avenging their leader's honor.

Jana kicked the lead man's knee, making him clench it with a hiss and fall.

The third man's hand clamped around her arm. He jerked her forward, and she knew his friends would jump her from behind. She twisted and kicked back at the man holding her, then rammed her elbow into his face. He let go, and Jana tried a flip that didn't quite get him to fall.

Instead, he staggered back, giving her the breathing space she needed to turn and face the other two men …

… and found she had no one left to fight. Her team had charged, wielding the tools they had been using to excavate the site. One of her would-be attackers got hit upside the head with the flat of a shovel, the metal making a long *clong*. The rest bolted, leaving their leader behind.

The fake archaeologist staggered to his feet. Despite being alone and outnumbered, he held her gaze.

"Don't think of trying to arrest me," he said. "I have friends who could make things very bad for you."

Her Moroccan foreman stepped forward, wielding a pick. Jana held up a hand.

"Let him go." She turned back to the antiquities thief. "You get to leave. But if you come back, or if anything in this dig gets touched, we'll call the police. Somebody take his photo."

Several students pulled out their phones and snapped pictures. The false professor cursed, turned on his heel, and stalked away.

Jana let out a long, slow breath. This dig had just gotten a whole lot more interesting.

CHAPTER FOUR

Jacob didn't like this assignment, but he had been on a lot of assignments he didn't like, so he gritted his teeth and drove his red Camaro at a satisfying hundred miles an hour along the seaside road to his bungalow on the coast just east of Athens. He had to pack. Of course he kept a bugout bag at headquarters in case he had to leave at a moment's notice, but he had a couple of hours before he needed to head to the airport so he had time to get ready properly.

Not that he was in a hurry.

The road grew narrow and winding. Jacob cut into the opposing lane to pass a slower car and wrenched the wheel as a truck came barreling around the corner, threatening to disintegrate him. The blare of a horn told him the trucker wasn't too happy with his little stunt.

Let him be unhappy. It wasn't like Jacob was happy either.

So Jana Peters was a doctor now. Well, a Ph.D. Not the kind of doctor he usually needed. Jana couldn't extract a bullet or set a broken limb.

Archaeology. He remembered—God, how long had it been?—her dad talking about her becoming an archaeologist. Way back then, judging from all the photos Paul had shown him, she had been a bookish kid barely out of her teens who couldn't decide on a major because every subject was so interesting to her.

That kid knew a lot about everything, except what her father did for a living. She was as in the dark as Gabriella, Jacob's on-again, off-again girlfriend.

It hadn't stayed that way, though, and that had broken her old man's heart.

Get the intel, and get the hell out of there. You don't need this crap. You got enough drama in your life.

Jacob cut hard onto a gravel road, his tires skidding, gravel scattering against the olive trees of the adjoining grove like a shotgun blast. He straightened the car out and shot down the road in a plume of dust.

A couple of hundred yards along, the road came to a stop at the end of a rocky promontory with a sweeping view of the glittering Mediterranean. On it stood a small house, its whitewashed walls and bay windows gleaming in the sun. The CIA's blood money could pay for a lot of life's luxuries.

Of course, appearances could be deceiving. This place was a fortress as much as a trophy home. The windows were made of double bulletproof glass, and the walls could take a hit from a rocket propelled grenade without cracking. Plus, technically it was the Company's property, not his.

He switched off the engine, hopped out, and hit a key code before he even tried putting a key in the door. That kept him from getting a spray of tear gas in the face. He unlocked both locks, then stepped quickly inside to punch in a second, different key code that kept an alarm from sounding at headquarters.

After that, he reactivated the tear gas, locked and bolted the door, and hit a button to raise the window blinds. As he strolled into the living room, the blinds rose to give him a sweeping view of the sea. Sailboats scudded along under a clear blue sky, and in the distance a cruise ship headed for the port.

Jacob stood there for a moment, staring out at the beauty, then went to the wet bar to one side of the room and mixed himself a strong Scotch and soda. Single malt, aged fifteen years. None of that blended, mass-produced crap.

Drink in hand, he moved to the bedroom and picked up his civilian phone.

He hadn't checked it in three weeks. Old Tyler Wallace, the perpetual worrier, had exaggerated. He hadn't been in Syria for a full month, and he'd enjoyed brief stays in Athens during his time in Iraq and Lebanon. Sometimes the Company had to extract him because the heat grew too much, and he'd come back on a different passport.

So he'd had some R and R. The result of that R and R had been calling him.

"Hey!" one text read, punctuated by hearts. "I'm in Athens next week for a photoshoot. I'd love to see you again."

Gabriella Cremonesi was an alluring Italian documentary and wildlife photographer he had met in Rome a few months back when he was investigating mob connections to the global arms network.

In her mid-twenties, she was a good ten years younger than him but had already won a couple of awards and got regular gigs from top-tier magazines and news agencies. She could just as easily have been on the other end of the camera as a fashion model. Jacob couldn't find a single flaw in her face or body, and he'd spent a good deal of time inspecting both.

He checked the date on the message. Two weeks ago. Damn, she'd be long gone.

"I'm in Liberia working with the refugees. Sorry," he had replied.

"That's so impressive. Your work must be so much more fulfilling than mine. I just document, while you make a real difference."

"Doctors without Borders are the real heroes. I'm just an administrator."

"You should be proud!"

"Your work is tough too. My Internet is spotty here. Not sure how often I can reply."

"Take care."

"You too, beautiful."

Jacob had written none of these things. His phone was hooked up to an AI that he could switch on and off. It allowed him to pretend to be around when he was out on a mission. His cover story of being an international aid worker in remote areas kept him from having to interact too much.

Gabriella had impressed Jacob with her utter lack of clinginess. She accepted Jacob's absences without question, and just as eagerly enjoyed his company when she could have it. In between, she had other lovers, just as Jacob did, and no loves, just like Jacob. No drama, no jealousy, no hint of a desire for commitment.

Jacob had just enough self-awareness to know that chasing around after women in their twenties would never land him in a long-term, serious relationship. Well, he didn't want one. Not only did he not have the time, but it would be seriously unfair to the other person. Long absences he couldn't explain without committing treason, and the very real chance that he might come back in a body bag, kept him from allowing himself to fall in love.

Besides, he didn't want to foist his emotional damage on somebody else, least of all someone he cared about, and despite his best efforts he did care about Gabriella. He tried to keep his relationships fun and superficial.

Another text from her was dated yesterday.

"Back in Athens. The agency needs some more pics of the general strike. Will be here for at least two days. Are you back?"

His finger hesitated over the text. She always stayed downtown and got a rental car. If she was free, there would be time for a quickie.

No, he decided, putting the phone away. That would be too superficial even for him. He'd do his intel gathering in Morocco, get the hell out as fast as possible, and then take some proper R and R like Wallace wanted him to.

He could fly back via Rome, or wherever Gabriella was at the moment, then return to Athens. Or maybe he could take her on that sailing trip around the islands they had been planning for months but never got the time to do. They could moor off one of the islands in the full moon, swim nude in the warm waters of the Mediterranean …

Enough. He had a plane to catch and a job to do.

Happiness was for other people.

CHAPTER FIVE

Dr. Jana Peters didn't realize her day was about to be ruined.

The dig was proceeding well. It had been three days since those looters had tried to con her out of her excavation, and they hadn't made a reappearance. She'd made a few calls to the authorities and now had a pair of uniformed policemen guarding the site at night. She had enough of a reputation and enough connections that she could swing that.

And the more she and her crew uncovered, the more enthusiastic they became. They'd expanded the test trench into regular squares in a grid pattern, each square measuring three-by-three meters. This made it easy to map the coordinates of the artifacts they found as well as features such as walls, doorways, and hearths.

The workers scraped the dirt away from these squares carefully with trowels, taking care to keep the soil level, as later finds got deposited in higher levels of soil called strata, with earlier deposits coming lower down. They had already cut through the late historic levels, finding a couple of stray potsherds and a bead of Berber design from the nineteenth century, before coming down on an occupation of squatters who had lived in the ruins of the villa in the fifth and sixth centuries. Those squatters, probably poor local famers, had left some rough pottery and a few badly corroded iron tools.

Soon her crew would scrape down enough to get as far as the test trench had gone—as far as the Roman villa itself. They were almost there, but they didn't hurry. Archaeology took time and care. Everything had to be recorded, because excavating a site essentially destroyed it.

The wait felt agonizing. She and the rest of the students and workers kept coming over to look at the portion of mosaic in the test trench. Soon, in a couple more days, they'd get down to it and reveal a work of ancient art unseen for almost two thousand years.

Jana smiled. She loved her job. She smiled further when she caught the eye of a certain graduate student. Brian was an older student who had spent a decade at a different career before pursuing his passion for the past. He was about her age, handsome, and obviously interested. Since he studied at a different university, there wouldn't be any impropriety, so maybe she'd take him up on that offer of a walk after the day's work was done.

Her smile turned into a concerned frown as she saw a Land Rover pull up on the dirt road a few hundred yards from the dig, on the same spot where those antiquities thieves had parked their vehicles.

A lone man got out. From this distance she couldn't see him clearly, but she could tell he was a well-built Anglo with short blonde hair wearing a wide-brimmed hat and loose khaki clothing. He walked toward her with a sense of purpose.

Jana gave a nervous glance at her crew and walked toward the man. She wanted to head him off before he caught a glimpse of that amazing mosaic, or the Roman gold coin a lucky undergraduate had uncovered that morning.

The fewer people who knew the details about her dig, the better.

Then Jana noticed the way he walked. The erect posture that spoke of a military background, and that strange, straight-armed manner of the right arm that didn't swing in time with his steps. That came from training. That came from someone who wanted to shave off a few milliseconds when drawing a gun.

Oh, crap. Who is this guy?

As she got closer, she studied the man's face. He looked familiar. Hard to tell at this distance, and those bruises were distracting. Maybe another group of archaeologists had kicked his ass for trying to steal their artifacts.

Then she stopped short as she finally recognized him.

She glared, crossing her arms.

"Well, well, well. The big brother I never knew."

"I'm not your brother," Jacob Snow said.

"Dad treated you like a son." *More than he treated me like a daughter.* "I heard all about you after he died. Saw all those pictures of you together."

"He was a good man."

The old grief came back, and the old jealousy.

"Why are you here?" Jana demanded.

"I need your help."

Jana glanced over her shoulder to make sure no one was approaching. A couple of the workers were looking curiously in their direction, but they had all stayed at the dig site, well out of earshot.

"I don't help the CIA," she said, lowering her voice just in case.

Jacob came up to her and stood there a moment.

"If I'm your brother, don't I get a hug?" he said, flashing a smile he probably thought could melt hearts. What an arrogant bastard. Like all of his kind.

"No."

"Your Canopic jar was stolen from Boston University a couple of days ago."

Jana jerked with surprise. "The fifth one?"

"I'm afraid so."

Her heart sank. The greatest find of her career.

"What happened, and why are you involved?"

"Let me show you." He pulled out his phone, brought up a video, and pressed play.

It showed security camera footage from outside a large stone building Jana instantly recognized as the museum. Blurry, as usual with that kind of camera, but clear enough. From above and from an angle, probably from an upper corner of the museum building, she watched a security guard standing by an entrance, not doing much of anything.

Suddenly he spun around, hand going to his gun. He paused, as if looking into the nearby shadows for the source of some sudden sound. A flash from the darkness and the man fell with a fatal headshot.

Jana winced. She'd seen plenty of death and suffering in her travels, but had never gotten used to it.

"A professional," Jacob said, seemingly unaffected. The bastard.

The intruder emerged from the darkness. Lean, muscular, moving with the grace of a feline. His face covered in a ski mask.

He? Yes. The shape of the body showed he was a male. The CCTV footage, while grainy, was clear enough for that.

The man went up to the door the security guard had been standing in front of and shot the lock off, then disappeared inside.

The view switched to a series of internal cameras as he ran up the stairs, obviously knowing exactly where he needed to go. Jana watched with increasing horror as he shot apart the display case, grabbed the jar, his movements expressing his surprise at how heavy it was, and then made his escape after gunning down a second innocent man.

The video ended.

"My God," Jana muttered.

"We think it was stolen by a terrorist group called The Sword of the Righteous. It's a splinter group of Al Qaeda. Like ISIS, they broke away because they think Al Qaeda isn't radical enough."

"I've heard of them. They kill a lot of foreign aid workers. Harvard had to shut down its work with the Iraqi National Museum because they were afraid of attacks. But why would they want a Canopic jar?"

"I was hoping you could tell me."

"I have no idea. I mean, it's worth millions since it's such a unique find, but you could say the same for several artifacts in that museum. And if they wanted it for its resale value on the illegal antiquities market, they should have stolen the whole set."

"Yeah. I did a little reading about Canopic jars. The four sons of Horus and all that. This was the only find where there was a fifth. So what's in it? Judging by the thief's movements, it's heavy."

"Fifty-two pounds. And we don't know what's in it. We did an x-ray and couldn't see through. Inside the alabaster there's a lining of lead."

"Why?"

"No idea."

"And you didn't open it?"

"Not yet. That's a decision for Boston University to make. So far they haven't made it. It's sealed so tight they're afraid they might break it. Also, they had a budget cut a while back and the funding for that project became low priority."

The same old story. Bean counters getting in the way of science.

"Anything else you can tell me about it?" Jacob asked. "The report mentioned an unusual inscription."

"A lot of Canopic jars have hieroglyphic inscriptions on their front, just below the head. One of the more common inscriptions on Canopic jars from the period reads, 'Thy bread is to thee. Thy beer is to thee. Thou livest upon that on which Ra lives.' Researchers normally interpret that as meaning that if all the spells in preparation of the dead are done right, then the deceased will have everything he or she needs in the afterlife. Four of the five Canopic jars from the burial had that inscription."

"And the fifth?" Jacob asked.

"It was a strange one. It read, 'The punishing power of Ra and Sekhmet destroys the enemies of Egypt.' That's not a typical inscription at all. For any period."

"Huh. And it's Sekhmet's head on that jar. I didn't get a chance to really look her up."

"Sekhmet is a lion-headed goddess and a daughter of Ra. She was often worshipped as a goddess of war because she personified the destructive power of her father, the sun. She was also the hot desert wind, brought pestilence, and breathed fire as hot as the sun."

"So the goddess of sunburn is guarding the punishing power of the sun. OK. But what does it all mean?"

Jana shrugged. "We don't know. I guess the terrorists will find out when they open it."

Jacob sighed, looking hesitant for a moment. That surprised her. CIA guys didn't usually allow cracks in their macho façade. Maybe getting beaten up had hurt his self-confidence. On second thought, probably not.

"This is disappointing. I hoped you'd have more to give me." He looked beyond her to the excavation. "You got a good assistant director?"

"Yes, an excellent Ph.D. student."

"Can he take over?"

"She. Why would she need to take over?"

"Because you need to come to Egypt with me."

"Egypt? Why?"

"Because that's where it was found. And chatter on the terrorist Dark Web indicates something big brewing in Egypt with The Sword of the Righteous."

She folded her arms and frowned. "I'm not going anywhere, not with you or any other CIA agent."

"Why not?" The guy looked genuinely baffled.

"You know why."

Jacob shook his head. "Jana, your father—"

"He never acted like my father."

"He loved you."

"Not as much as he loved you," Jana snapped. "He spent more time with you than his own daughter, or even his aging parents."

"You got him wrong. And this mission is serious, really serious, or I wouldn't have come to speak with you."

"Well, you've spoken with me. Now get lost, and don't contact me again."

Jana stormed off back to the dig. Jacob didn't follow.

Well, in a way he did. Her phone buzzed. It was a message from him with his contact information.

How did he know her private phone number?

Stupid question. The CIA knew everything. No privacy. No respect for personal life.

It was one of the many, many things she hated about the CIA.

Now she was twice as convinced that she wasn't going off with Jacob Snow.

CHAPTER SIX

Institute for Nuclear Physics
Johannes Gutenberg-Universität, Mainz, Germany
That same day

Professor Klaus Meyer walked out the front door of the Institute for Nuclear Physics, smiling happily to himself. His research was going well, thanks in no small part to a brilliant Japanese postdoc he had just hired. Together they were exploring more efficient ways of splitting atoms, a procedure that promised one day to make the power input requirement for nuclear power plants a tenth of what it was today.

"To make energy, first you must spend energy," he always told his students. Well, with a few years' more work, that equation would become much more cost-effective.

Doctor Meyer was a strong public advocate of nuclear energy. The field had gotten a bad rap thanks to Hiroshima, Nagasaki, and the threat of mutually assured destruction during the Cold War. Then there were disasters like Chernobyl and Fukushima.

What people didn't realize was that those were antiquated designs. Fukushima was built in 1967. Chernobyl was built in 1972, and by a Communist regime that prioritized production quotas over safety. The latest generation of designs was far more efficient and far, far safer. It promised clean, cheap energy that could solve the climate crisis. Despite what people thought, solar and wind could never be scaled up enough to support eight billion people. Nuclear was the only viable option.

And as for using nuclear weapons, no sane country would do that. America and the Soviet Union had been at each other's throats for sixty years and had never dared. As corrupt and narcissistic as world leaders could be, they all valued their lives. Pushing the button put themselves at risk as much as anyone else. Those in charge of the world's nuclear arsenal were sane enough never to use them as anything more than deterrents.

He walked through the university's campus, its ultramodern buildings of glass and steel softened by green lawns and spreading trees. Doctor Meyer saw none of it, lost as he was in mathematical equations and dreams of the future.

Just as he crossed one of the streets intersecting the campus, a loud boom snapped him out of his reverie.

He jerked his head around and saw smoke billowing up from a few buildings away.

"That looks like the university chapel!" he exclaimed.

People screamed. Students and faculty began to run away from the blast. The smoke puffed up into the blue sky.

With all the noise, Doctor Meyer didn't even notice the van screeching to a halt beside him until the back opened up and a pair of masked men leapt out and grabbed him.

"Hey!"

A fist to his paunchy stomach cut off any more objection. The men bundled him into the van, where a third man gagged and bound him with duct tape. He did this with quick, practiced motions, so rapidly that he finished before the other two had slammed the back doors shut.

The van peeled out, making Doctor Meyer fall over. One of his abductors righted him and, hyperventilating, he looked around.

While they all wore ski masks, he could see the brown eyes and dusky skin. When one spoke to the other in what sounded like Arabic, Doctor Meyer's worst fears were realized.

Terrorists. I've been abducted by terrorists.

Campus security had discussed this possibility with him, and together they had gone through the security features of the institute. They had even been so kind as to install a state-of-the-art burglar alarm in his house.

But they hadn't anticipated terrorists setting off a bomb as a distraction and then grabbing him as he walked between buildings.

They got me.

But I'm not the only one.

He spotted a trembling woman sitting on the other side of the van, bound and gagged like he was.

Meyer stared at her a moment. She looked familiar. It took a moment to place her.

Professor Inge Weber of the archaeology department. He had only met her once, at an interdepartmental mixer, and wouldn't have recalled her name at all if she hadn't been in the campus paper just last week talking about the results of her recent excavation in Egypt.

An Egyptologist? Why would terrorists abduct an Egyptologist?

31

Jana Peters stared at her phone message, her stomach sick with horror and disbelief.

It was from a German colleague, telling her the horrible news that Professor Inge Weber, a friend and one of her closest colleagues, had been abducted in a suspected terrorist strike.

Weber was an expert on the hieroglyphs of the Late and Greco-Roman Periods of Egypt, and had translated the inscriptions in the catacombs where they had found the mysterious set of five Canopic jars.

She called Jacob, her reluctance to deal with him forgotten. Now all that mattered was helping Inge.

He picked up on the second ring.

"Jacob, did you hear about the terror attack at the Johannes Gutenberg-Universität in Mainz?"

"Yeah. They took an Egyptologist and a nuclear physicist. We don't have much intel yet but it's probably The Sword of the Righteous. The woman was associated with your dig, right?"

"Yeah. Wait, they took a nuclear physicist too? Why would they do that?"

"Should be obvious." That made Jana roll her eyes. Typical CIA arrogance. All of Dad's coworkers had acted like that. "Why they'd kidnap an Egyptologist after stealing an ancient artifact is the real question."

"Wait. Do you think they might come after me?"

"I'm sure they'd like to, but at far as we know The Sword of the Righteous doesn't have a branch in Morocco. King Mohammed VI has been pretty good at stamping out that sort of crap. Wish I could say the same about his neighbors. Hell, wish I could say the same about Europe. They might have been planning to grab you but couldn't reach you."

"Oh my God. We've got to help them."

"You on board?"

Jana rubbed her temples. "Yeah, I'm on board. But where do we start?"

"I hate to admit it, but we're stuck. And when I'm stuck, I always go back to the beginning. That means Egypt. This seems to center around Egypt anyway. I say we go check out your dig site."

"When I'm stuck, I always go back to the beginning."

That's what Dad always used to say.

Damn right I'm stuck. Stuck with you, Jacob.
Stuck with the CIA.

CHAPTER SEVEN

Captain Arnold Cranston stood at the helm of the *USS Brandywine*, a Ticonderoga-class guided-missile cruiser, as it moved through the Strait of Gibraltar from the Atlantic to the western Mediterranean. Arrayed around it were two destroyers and five littoral combat ships, including two vessels specifically designed for antisubmarine action.

They'd need those once they got where they were going. Iran had a fleet of 34 subs, some of pretty recent design. That could cause some serious havoc to the fleet that was assembling to add muscle to the current political showdown.

Iran had just conducted one of its "elections," a semi-sham in which only a few political parties could run. Since the imams, headed by the unelected Supreme Leader, had more power over policy than the civilian government, it didn't matter much who won the elections anyway.

Still, the hardliners had freaked out when a reformer got elected president and his party gained a majority in the legislature.

During his campaign, Ali Bagheri had promised to "reset" his nation's relationship with the West, hinting that Iran's nuclear program was negotiable, and he had even claimed that "our esteemed Islamic sisters need to make their own choices in life."

Of course, this had all been couched in fiery rhetoric and a fair amount of nationalist chest-thumping, but it was the most progressive stance of any major Iranian political figure in decades.

And it had won him the election. Iran's young population, enjoying few economic opportunities and, thanks to the Internet, knowing exactly what they were missing if they lived in a more open country, had voted for him in droves.

So the hardliners had done the only thing they knew how to do—create a false crisis to hang onto power. They had abducted a team of American citizens—art historians and photographers, of all people—and put them up on bogus espionage charges. They were with a New York publisher that specialized in coffee table books on the great cities of the world, and had been covering Isfahan's remarkable Safavid architecture with no trouble for a good three weeks when the Revolutionary Guard decided they were spies.

No one, simply no one, believed that. Well, maybe some of the crazier of Iran's crazies, but no one with half a brain. Crowds of university students had even protested in Isfahan and Tehran for their release. That had freaked out the hardliners even more.

So now the U.S. and Iran were at a standoff. Sanctions. Harsh words. Rallying of support among America's allies. Tepid speeches from the United Nations. The Revolutionary Guard held firm. They said the elections had been rigged by a Zionist conspiracy and they had demanded a recount.

Now the Supreme Leader and the imams had taken control until the "recount" could be finished. Ali Bagheri and several key members of his party were under house arrest "for their protection."

Negotiation had gone nowhere. So now came the time for a show of force. Ships from all over were converging on the Persian Gulf to reinforce America's naval power there. The *USS Brandywine* and her escort vessels were among them, detached just the day before from the Atlantic fleet.

At maximum speed, it would take two and a half days to get to the Suez Canal, and a similar amount of time to round the Arabian Peninsula and join the gathering fleet in the Persian Gulf.

The *USS Brandywine* would be the last large ship to make it, but what it carried on the warheads of some of its Tomahawk missiles made it the most important ship of all.

Captain Cranston prayed every night before going to bed that he wouldn't have to use those warheads.

The captain kept a careful eye on both sides of the strait, asking for constant updates from his radar technician. He hated sailing through narrow channels. Anyone who had studied the great naval defeats of history knew how dangerous they could be.

To the north lay the coast of Spain, visible as rugged hills topped with wind farms. Spain was an ally. No trouble there, at least not from the authorities. To the south lay the cliffs of Morocco, the port of Tangier just becoming visible ahead. Morocco was an ally in the war on terror, but couldn't be relied on for anything else since they were in one of their regular pissing matches with Spain about that country's two enclaves in North Africa. Beyond, on the north coast, lay Gibraltar, still in British hands after all these years. A friendly port offering naval and air backup if needed.

Despite his caution, Cranston was more worried about the next bottleneck he and his flotilla would have to go through—the Suez

Canal. At least Egypt was an ally, the military junta being America's best ally in the Middle East after Israel.

That wasn't good enough to make him feel secure. A few years before, the radical Muslim Brotherhood had won the elections, bringing in a host of restrictive laws, oppressing the nation's large Christian population, and even threatening Israel.

So the military had staged a coup, banned the Muslim Brotherhood, and ran elections that they won easily since the Muslim Brotherhood was the only other large political party.

The generals were now firmly in control, but the Suez Canal was still fraught with danger. A narrow channel, 120 miles long, flanked mostly by open countryside, there were countless points where a terrorist could launch a missile attack on the fleet, which would be strung out and moving slowly, making the perfect target.

A branch of ISIS operated in the Sinai Peninsula to the east of the canal, and he had just been sent intel that a new group, The Sword of the Righteous, was planning some sort of attack in Egypt, most likely on the American embassy.

Back home, the pundits and talking heads worried about a war with Iran. Captain Cranston felt like he was getting into the warzone early—as soon as he entered the Suez Canal.

Two and a half days. Two and a half days before he was a sitting duck in between two active terrorist organizations.

CHAPTER EIGHT

Jacob Snow kept his eyes open.

They were in Egypt, in a stretch of cultivated fields just to the west of Alexandria, the nation's biggest Mediterranean port at the end of the broad Nile Delta. Jana Peters was leading him to her old dig site.

They walked down a narrow dirt track bounded on both sides by farmland. Tough peasants dressed in headscarves and djellabas tilled the earth or cleared silt from the complex system of small irrigation channels that crisscrossed the land, keeping the ground damp under a punishing sun. Apparently no one had told Sekhmet it was winter. The humidity the Delta gave off didn't help, and Jacob's shirt stuck to his back.

It was peaceful here, isolated. The Delta was one of Egypt's more prosperous regions, but that didn't mean radical Islamists hadn't managed to get their claws into the local hearts and minds.

The farmers stared at them as they passed. Foreigners were rare in these parts, there being no obvious tourist sites and the last paved road being a mile back. They had to park their rental Jeep and walk to get here.

Jacob hated sticking out like this. It made him feel like a target.

"It's just ahead," Jana told him.

Jacob couldn't see much except a low, rocky outcrop about the size of a football field with a chain-link fence around it. A small concrete shed stood near the center.

His hand strayed to the shoulder holster hidden under his light khaki vest. A local operative had met him at their hotel in Alexandria, giving him a 9mm pistol and a couple of stun grenades.

The operative hadn't been able to come along.

"Sorry, but I've got to investigate some chatter about some terrorists infiltrating the port," he had said.

"The Sword of the Righteous?" Jacob had asked.

"We're not sure. I'll keep you updated."

So here he was, poorly armed, in the middle of nowhere, with a civilian woman in tow. Great. Just freaking great.

"So Jana, you told me it was a set of catacombs. Tell me what we can expect."

"The Delta is mostly damp silt laid down by the Nile, but there are several naturally occurring islands of rock scattered around it. We're coming up on one of them. Starting in the Greek period, after Alexander the Great conquered Egypt, the locals began to dig catacombs in them to bury their dead. The Egyptians were obsessed with preserving their bodies for the afterlife, and so they didn't want to get buried in this soil."

"Didn't the Greeks come with their own religion?" Those nude statues were the only part of history class he had paid attention to in high school.

"They did, but they took on Egyptian ways pretty quickly. They dug multilevel catacombs, some of which spread for miles. They continued to be used in the Roman period."

"And you discovered this one?"

"We did."

The note of pride was obvious in her voice. Jacob had never been into all this stuff, but finding an ancient catacomb sounded pretty cool, especially for some civilian academic like her.

How different she is from her old man.

"So what's the entrance like? What are the tunnels and rooms like?"

"One armed guard at the entrance. Hired by an Egyptian colleague. He can be trusted. The entrance is behind a locked metal door. Beyond that is a spiral ramp cut out of living rock leading to four levels of catacombs. No electric light, that's why I had you buy flashlights. The corridors are narrow and some of the ceilings are unstable. Plenty of places to hide, plus we haven't fully examined all the areas or opened all the tombs. The lowest level is half flooded with ground water and totally unstable."

Jacob nodded. Not a bad tactical assessment for a civilian. Perhaps the old man had worn off on her a bit after all.

Aaron Peters. He taught me a hell of a lot too.

Jacob shook himself. No time for reminiscing. He was on a mission.

"You all right?" Jana asked.

"What do you mean?"

"You shook all over for a moment."

"Loosening up."

Jana eyed him but didn't reply. They came to the rock outcropping. A middle-aged Egyptian man with an old rifle slung over his shoulder appeared from around the concrete shed.

"Doctor Peters, is that you?" he called out in Arabic.

"Yes, Mohammed," Jana replied in the same language. "How is your family?"

"Fine, praise be to Allah. And how is yours?"

The traditional greeting made Jana's features tighten, just for a moment, then she replied, "All fine, praise be to God."

Several more traditional greetings continued as Mohammed opened the gate, inquiries after each other's health, neighbors, the grades Mohammed's children were getting at school, etc. Jacob had long been amused at how the people of the Middle East could have an entire conversation and never get beyond some variation of "hello." Charming, in a way, but not when you were in a hurry.

He had to hold in his impatience as Jana introduced him as a fellow archaeologist and they went through a second round of traditional greetings. At least they staved off the invitation to tea, a ritual that would last at least half an hour.

"Afterwards, Mohammed," Jana said. "Has anyone been around?"

"No. Just a man from the Antiquities Department yesterday to take a look at the ceilings. Some more cracks have developed on the third level."

"That's too bad. My colleague and I have to check on a few things."

"Take care if you go to the lower levels."

Mohammed unlocked a flimsy metal door and they entered the shed's cool, dank interior. The guard remained outside.

As Jacob's eyes adjusted, he could see the black hole of what looked like a well some ten feet across, except around it a stone ramp spiraled downwards. They turned on their flashlights, Jacob stepped over to the edge and shone his beam down.

He couldn't see the bottom. All he could see was the ramp spiraling down, and a low stone wall at waist height protecting anyone from falling in.

They descended, their footsteps echoing. Jacob felt a chill, not entirely from the cool air wafting up from below. He had been afraid of the dark when he was small, and every now and then a little bit of that came back.

Like in the caves of Tora Bora, hiding out from the Taliban in the darkness as he heard the whispered voices of those who wanted to cut his throat.

No.

He didn't have time for a flashback right now.

"The upper levels are stable," Jana said.

Jacob felt a spike of irritation. Had she said that because she thought he was nervous? Did she have any idea what he really did at the CIA?

Further down, they saw a dark opening on the side wall.

"That's a dining room," Jana said.

"Excuse me?"

"Relatives of the deceased would come and eat a meal with their spirit."

"In the middle of a bunch of corpses? Damn, and I thought fast food was unhealthy."

"No, the corpses are further down."

She said this in a blasé manner, as if to impress him.

I've seen way more corpses than you have, honey, not that I wanted to. I'd rather have your innocence than my experience.

Way too late for that, though.

Jacob shone his light into the room as they passed and saw a bare chamber, perhaps ten feet by twenty, with low benches around the side like he had seen in paintings of ancient dining rooms. He imagined the ancient Greeks, and later Romans, reclining there on cushions, eating grapes and sipping wine while their relatives moldered a few levels below.

"So what are we looking for?" Jana asked as they continued down.

"I don't know. Whatever you might have missed the first time. You said there were unexplored sections?"

"There are four levels. The lowest level is partially filled with groundwater and the ceiling is unstable. The second lowest level is in pretty bad shape too. We didn't spend much time in either of them. We're coming on the first level now."

A side passage led out of sight. To either side, Jacob could see niches in the walls like shelves, each about six feet long. He didn't need to be an archaeologist to know what they had once contained.

Jacob stopped. "You mapped and studied this place pretty well, right?"

"The top two levels, yes. We didn't find much. It got looted in antiquity. These niches were originally covered with carved slabs. Those got broken by the ancient looters. We only found a few artifacts. The second floor had more. Let's go down there."

"All right."

They continued down the ramp to another doorway opening onto a passageway that looked much like the last one. It ran straight, beyond the reach of their flashlights, a couple of side passages branching off.

The walls were lined with niches that had once contained bodies, the floor littered with smashed slabs of stone. Inside one of the nearby niches, Jacob saw a few shreds of mummy wrappings.

"There's an inscription down the hall I want to take a second look at," Jana said.

Once again, Jacob felt a prickle of fear run up his spine.

Don't be a baby. You're not five anymore.

They went down the hall, having to step over the debris, their footsteps echoing in the dark expanse. The cool air gave him goosebumps. Jacob spotted one slab that was more intact than the rest. A cracked stone face of a woman in bas-relief stared up at them with blank eyes. Jacob looked away.

"Here, down this side passage," the archaeologist said.

They turned right, and saw a hallway much like the one they had just left, running out of reach of their flashlights.

Damn, how big is this place?

You could get lost in here no problem. Keep walking and walking ...

It was nice to have someone to hold in the dark. He wished Gabriella was here.

To his shock, Jacob noticed a couple of the slabs remained in place. One was blank except for an inscription in Greek. The other had a carving of a man and woman, him wearing a tunic and holding a sword, her wearing loose robes and holding something he couldn't identify, standing side by side and looking out at him.

A man and wife, buried together for all time. They spent their life together and now they're spending an eternity together.

Not for you, Jacob old buddy.

"Here," Jana said. Her voice had gone down to a whisper.

On a portion of the wall between two niches, one of which still had some jumbled bones in it, some ancient scribe had carved a series of hieroglyphics.

"Why are they writing in ancient Egyptian? There's a Greek inscription right over there."

"They used both. It was a fascinating example of cultural melding."

Fascinating. Just tell me what the terrorists are looking for so I can neutralize them.

Jana ran her finger along the carving, or rather just over the carving. Even though it was of stone, she seemed to treat it like it was delicate glass. Jacob worried more about the ceilings. He could see a crack right above them.

41

"I wish I had my notes with me. Inge translated this. It said something about the light of Ra. Let me see, hieroglyphics aren't my specialty."

She began to mutter to herself, staring at the picture writing in the light of her flashlight.

"I thought you were an Egyptologist."

"I specialize in the Roman period. It takes me all over. Please don't interrupt when I'm concentrating."

Well excuse the hell out of me.

After a moment, she read aloud, "Entombed along this wall are the priests of the sacred punishing light of Ra and Sekhmet, the invisible light that burns and makes one sick."

"It says that?"

"I think so. Or something pretty close. It takes a decade to get truly fluent. I'm half remembering what Inge translated it as in the field report."

"That does sound like what was on the Canopic jar. But what the hell does it mean?"

Jana answered with a shrug.

A shout echoed through the dark corridors, sending a shiver up Jacob's spine.

"What was that?"

"It sounded like Mohammed's voice," Jana said.

Then came a sound Jacob was much more familiar with.

The sound of a gunshot.

CHAPTER NINE

Jacob turned off his flashlight. Jana was smart enough to do the same without having to be told, plunging the catacombs into Stygian darkness. Jacob shuddered, glad this irritating woman couldn't see. He pulled out his gun. That made him feel better. Not enough, but some.

The echo of the gunshot took a long time to die down. Jacob swore he heard the patter of dust and grit falling from the ceiling somewhere nearby.

Then he heard something else—voices and footsteps. Several people were speaking at the same time, the multiple voices and their echoes blending the words to make them impossible to follow, and yet he could distinctly hear that some German was mixed in with the Arabic.

It couldn't be the hostages from the university attack, could it?

A hell of a coincidence, but it made sense. Just like he had come back to the beginning to figure out what was going on, it looked like the terrorists had too, and they had brought their hostages with them.

At least Mohammed had died without telling his killers they were down here. That gave them a chance.

The footsteps and voices grew louder. The darkness paled. A faint light illuminated the vaguest outlines of the hallway Jacob and Jana stood in. The terrorists were moving down the ramp.

The light waxed, and for a tense moment Jacob felt sure they would head straight for the inscription Jana had just read, but then the light faded again.

"They're going to the lower levels," Jana whispered so faintly he almost didn't catch the words.

Jacob turned his flashlight around in his hand until his palm covered the lens. Then he turned it on. Only a little light filtered around his hand, just enough to see where to put his feet and not enough that the terrorists, bathed in their own light, would notice.

"Stay here," he whispered. "I'm going to follow them."

"Hell, no. I'm going with you."

"You sure aren't."

"This is a maze. You'll get lost, and there are some passages that are really unstable. I need to be with you to warn you which ones."

Jacob thought for a moment, cursed silently, and said, "All right. Let's go. But once you lead me to them, you get the hell out of here. All right?"

"All right."

Jacob studied her for a moment with the thin light of his flashlight, unsure that she was telling the truth. He noticed she had tears in her eyes.

"What's the matter?"

"Mohammed. I know his family." Her voice cracked.

Jacob blinked. He was so accustomed to death that sometimes he forgot how it affected other people.

He paused for a moment, then said, "I'll avenge him."

"That won't bring him back," she whispered.

Jacob had nothing to say to that.

They walked along the passageway with care, keeping their eyes on their feet and stepping high over the debris. In the shifting shadow of his covered flashlight, that funeral slab with the ancient woman's face seemed to take on life, peering at them with stony eyes that seemed to follow them as they passed.

They got to the corner and peeked down the next passageway, the one that led to the central ramp. The lights from the terrorist group had almost faded out.

"They're not on the ramp anymore," Jana whispered.

"Which level do you think they went to?"

"Only one way to find out."

They walked as quickly as possible to the ramp and saw a faint glow coming from far below. They heard distant voices and a splash of water.

"They're in the lowest level," Jana whispered.

Damn. If it's half filled with water, that's going to make it hard to sneak up on them.

They continued down the ramp, passing more side passages on the third level. The darkness didn't bother Jacob so much anymore. When he knew of a threat, he felt more confident than when there was simply the possibility of a threat.

I sure made the Taliban afraid of the dark.

Them and my own side.

Focus!

Although they were further down now, the light below had grown fainter, as if the terrorists had gone further into the labyrinth.

A loud splash and a shout made them freeze.

44

There was a distant babble of voices, muffled a bit by the echo. A woman shouted something in German. While Jacob spoke the language, he couldn't make out the words.

"That sounded like Inge's voice," Jana whispered.

"Did you catch what she said?"

"I think she was saying the ceiling was going to fall."

Great.

"Let's go," he muttered.

He tightened his grip on the front of his flashlight, dimming the light to the point that they could barely see the floor directly beneath their feet. Jacob didn't dare let it shine more, though, in case one of the terrorists stood watch a bit behind the main group.

A faint sparkle up ahead told him they were almost to the water line. Another splash and a clearly shouted Arabic curse told him the terrorists were still having problems with the ceiling.

Sure can't use my stun grenades in this combat environment.

Jacob located the sound as coming from a passageway to their left. He could see a dim glow, making the water in the passage ripple with a fairy light. He also saw passages going ahead and to the right. Apparently the ramp ended here in a circular room.

He stepped into the water, feeling it chill his legs up to his knees. Slowly he waded along, trying not to make much noise although movement in complete silence proved impossible. Jana kept right by him. He felt tempted to tell her to stay behind, but it looked like she had spoken the truth. This really was a maze. He didn't want to get lost in here.

The question was, given how flooded and unstable it was, how well did she know it herself? Had the archaeologists dared to go much beyond the landing?

Jacob and Jana came to the entrance to the hallway and Jacob turned off his flashlight. Thanks to the terrorists, he had enough light to see where he was going.

Ahead of him stretched a long corridor, its damp walls gleaming in the feeble light. Grave niches appeared as black rectangles on either wall. A couple remained covered by their funerary slabs, adorned with ghostly stone faces.

About fifty yards ahead, he could see the hallway branched into a four-way intersection. The light shone strongest from the righthand corridor. Voices echoed down to him. They spoke German, a man demanding, a woman pleading. He could see ripples in the water at the intersection from the terrorists and their captives moving around.

Jacob motioned for Jana to stay behind him, and slowly he advanced, gun leveled, flashlight ready to switch on to glare in the eyes of any terrorist who came around the corner.

He stumbled over some submerged debris, gritting his teeth as he made a soft splash. The black water rippled ahead of him as far as the intersection, mingling with the ripples made by the terrorists.

Jacob paused a moment, letting the ripples calm, and then moved forward again, feeling his way with care. His slow speed frustrated him to no end, but to hurry now might mean losing everything.

Jana followed. He had wanted her to stay put. He waved his hand at her again, motioning her back, but she kept coming.

Not daring to have a whispered argument this close to the target, he continued forward. Each step created a slight ripple. If any of The Sword of the Righteous looked at the intersection, they might figure out they weren't the only ones disturbing the water.

Nothing he could do about that except hope. He kept going, painfully slowly, hoping they didn't kill the two scientists.

As he drew closer, he could make out the German conversation.

"I don't understand why you want me to translate hieroglyphs. What do you want from them?" the woman said.

"Just do as you're told, you filthy unbeliever. It's all I can do to keep myself from cutting your head off and sharing the video online. You think I haven't done that before? I have done it, lots of times. The last time was some stupid European woman like you who worked for the Red Cross. Look! I'll cut you with this!"

He must have produced a weapon because the woman screamed.

"All right! All right!" she cried. "Let me concentrate."

Jacob spared a brief glance over his shoulder to check on Jana, only visible as a shadow behind him. Despite the threat to her friend, she looked like she was keeping her cool. Good. Most civilians would freak out in this situation.

Well, she is Aaron Peters's daughter. She's got it in the blood.

While only two people had spoken, Jacob could faintly hear the movements of more people, and the ripples coming from around the corner made him estimate a small group of perhaps half a dozen.

About the same size as the group that witnesses said kidnapped Professors Meyer and Weber.

They must have a hell of a network to all get here so quickly without being detected. The Sword of the Righteous must have been building up for years before they made themselves known.

Professor Inge Weber's voice said in a wavering voice, "The lead seal of Ra contains the sacred punishing light of Ra and Sekhmet, the invisible light that burns and makes one sick."

"Perfect!" another male voice said in Arabic. "You hear what the infidel bitch said? It's exactly what we thought."

Still Jacob crept forward. To his right he saw a niche with a decayed skeleton. To his left an intact grave slab showing a mournful male face. His steps grew uncertain. Debris had piled up here, small stones slipping under his feet. A quick glance upwards showed him deep fissures in the ceiling surrounded by spiderwebs of smaller cracks.

Almost to the intersection. Jacob relaxed, his training kicking in. Nothing mattered now. Not the darkness he had never stopped fearing, not the annoying woman behind him, not the fact that he was outnumbered probably six to one in a hostage situation.

All that mattered was the mission, and Jacob Snow always completed the mission.

Just a few more steps, and he'd duck around the corner, blind them with his flashlight and, if the positioning was right, take out all the terrorists without the hostage getting hurt.

A tall order, but he'd done it before and he'd do it again. All he needed was surprise.

And he lost that when a sharp crackling sounded above him. He paused and looked up, just in time to get hit in the shoulder by a chunk of ceiling the size of a cantaloupe.

The impact made him drop his flashlight, which let out a brief flash of light before shorting out when it dropped beneath the water's surface.

Jana cried out as Jacob fell to his knees in the icy water.

Before he could get up, he heard a chorus of shouts and a loud splashing. The bright beams of several flashlights pointed at the intersection.

CHAPTER TEN

Jacob burst into motion. He leapt up and forward to get to the intersection first. If he could, he'd be able to use the corner for cover while the terrorists would be exposed in the hallway. If he couldn't, the roles would be reversed and he and Jana would be dead in a matter of seconds.

The sound of splashing just around the corner told him he wasn't going to make it.

"Take cover!"

He shouted this as he dove into the water.

That probably saved his life, because the next moment one of the terrorists came around the corner and opened up. Even underwater he heard the rapid fire of the automatic pistol as clear as day.

Jana's dead. After all the CIA put her through and now I've gotten her killed.

Rage rose up in him like lava spewing from a volcano. He kicked off from the floor, swimming underwater with powerful strokes, ignoring the ache in his shoulder.

He collided with the terrorist, wrapped his arms around his legs and, planting his own feet, rose up, lifting the man up with him and tossing him in what he hoped was the direction of his buddies.

Before he even had time to wipe his eyes, he fired three shots blind, then leapt backwards.

His back collided with the wall, bringing down a shower of rock fragments from the ceiling. He wiped his eyes with the back of his free hand and, in the two seconds before the water streaming down his face obscured his vision again, saw one man disappear below the surface and another man leaning against the opposite wall, clutching his bloody abdomen.

Jacob had ended up at one corner of the intersection, not quite being able to see down the passageway where the remaining terrorists stood. He backpedaled as another one rounded the corner, gun at the ready.

A shot to the head took the guy out.

Someone shouted something in Arabic that he couldn't catch over the ringing in his ears. A moment later, all of the Arabs' flashlights went out, plunging the labyrinth into darkness. Jacob's own flashlight had fallen into the water and, not being waterproof, had shorted out. The same must have happened to Jana's.

He heard splashing. It sounded like the terrorists running away.

Jacob stepped forward, heart beating fast, his gun leveled and his free hand groping for the wall.

A rush of water below him. He felt strong arms wrap around his middle, and then felt himself get lifted up. One of the members of The Sword of the Righteous was using Jacob's own trick against him.

I hate a fast-learning enemy, Jacob thought as he got flung against the wall, smacking his head.

The impact brought another cascade of stones down. One must have hit his invisible opponent, because his grip loosened.

That's all the opening Jacob needed. He brought the heel of his palm up, aiming for where he guessed the man's chin to be.

Almost guessed right. Instead he felt it connect with the soft tissue of the guy's nose.

There's an urban legend that if you hit the nose just right it will drive the bone right through the brain and kill your opponent. He had learned in basic training that this is false. The nose doesn't have a bone, it has much softer cartilage which simply crumples with enough impact.

Still, it's enough to stun a man, enough for Jacob to grab this particular man, knee him in the stomach, and push him under the water.

Jacob dove down too, getting him in a chokehold and keeping only his own head above water. He wouldn't put it past one of these crazies to blindly open up with a machine gun. That would probably bring the whole damn ceiling down but hey, at least the idiot would get his 72 virgins.

The man he had in a chokehold struggled, but Jacob kept him down, his powerful arm keeping the terrorist's neck in a vice grip. The guy scrabbled at Jacob's arm, couldn't pull it away, and got smart.

He went for Jacob's balls.

Jacob felt the guy grabbed for them, miss, and get his inner thigh. The terrorist got a good handful on his second try. Jacob hissed in pain and twisted his hips to pull away.

Big mistake. A pain that heralded at least a week's abstinence shot through his midsection. He gasped and toppled over, his head going under. Still he kept the terrorist in a chokehold as the man made desperate attempts to wriggle free.

Those attempts grew weaker and weaker. Jacob got his head and gun above the surface again and heard splashing coming from both directions.

Damn, were this asshole's friends zeroing in on him?

The splashing grew louder as his opponent's struggles grew weaker and finally stopped altogether. The sound came mostly from his right, the direction he had come, assuming he hadn't become completely disoriented. And it sounded close.

Giving the man he held underwater a final squeeze to the neck, he let him go, trailing his fingers along his back to make sure he sank to the bottom and didn't suddenly try to get away. No. He was dead.

Jacob leveled his gun in the direction he had heard the splashing, eyes straining at the utter blackness. It sounded distant now. They were moving away? Or was that a second person moving through the water?

"Now!" came a distant shout in Arabic that echoed like the cry of a spirit through the subterranean chambers. There was a soft splash near him. Jacob adjusted his aim, still not sure he was on target.

A source of light came on in the direction he had come. It was faint, the shine illuminating the passageway but not revealing the source, which appeared to be around the corner in the central chamber. He saw no one between him and it. So what had that other splash been? Unless that dark circle low in the water …

… he had no time for that now, because an instant later the second source flashed on, focused right on him.

It came from the corridor where he had seen the terrorists.

A shot blared through the confined space. Jacob was already dodging. He felt the heat of the bullet as it passed by his head to smack into the funerary slab of the grave behind him. It was followed by a rush of water and suddenly two dark figures descended on him.

Jacob brought up his gun but his hand got knocked to the side and his shot buried itself in the ceiling, bringing down several stones.

It would have been nice if they had fallen on the terrorists' heads, but Jacob Snow had never been a lucky man. He felt his wrist clamped in an iron grip, his gun forced to the side as a fist slammed into his face.

His attackers were silhouettes, illuminated by a third man with a flashlight just behind. The light glared in Jacob's eyes, but he could still see the gleam of a knife in the second man's hand.

That knife moved in for the kill.

Jacob pulled back and to the right, and the knife missed him by inches. The man who had him in his grip clamped down on his shoulder with his free hand, trying to immobilize him so his partner could gut him.

Jacob rammed his fist into the man's armpit, dislocating his shoulder and making him let go. The knife slashed at him; Jacob, forced to back away again, tripped over some submerged rubble and fell into the water with a splash.

He kicked away to get some distance, then rose to fire.

The knifeman was right on him. Jacob put three bullets into his gut, then a fourth into the other man's head. That brought another cascade of dust and small stones from the ceiling.

A light glared on him from the other direction. Jacob was caught like a deer between the headlights of two oncoming cars.

Jacob plunged into the water as a fusillade of shots sought him out. He felt a shift in the current, perhaps from a heavy stone getting dropped from the ceiling.

Damn. If this keeps up we're all going to get buried.

He stayed underwater, keeping himself submerged by holding onto a heavy stone resting on the floor. The lights shone around the area he had been, the beams diffused by the dust swirling in the water. He stayed still, hoping not to be seen.

His lungs began to burn as the lights continued to seek him out. Then they began to withdraw.

A trick? His lungs wouldn't allow him to wait any more. He hadn't been able to get a breath before diving. Jacob moved a bit to the right and brought his head above water. He blinked the water away, trying desperately to see.

"Did we get him?" a man's voice asked in Arabic.

"Get off me!" a woman shouted in Arabic. That was Jana's voice! How the hell had she survived?

"Shut up," the same voice snapped. "You have the professor?"

"Yes," a second male voice said.

Jacob brought up his gun. He had shifted until he was right in the intersection, keeping his head low. Two flashlight beams cut paths through the darkness, but they had withdrawn several yards down their respective hallways. Jacob hoped that with the rippling water and crazy shadows from the wavering beams that they wouldn't spot him.

"There!"

Jacob dove under the water again as a second fusillade hammered away around him. He felt a strong displacement of water and a shaking all around him that even underwater he could hear as an ominous rumble.

The whole corridor sounded like it was collapsing, and the terrorists had both the German Egyptologist and Jana.

CHAPTER ELEVEN

Jacob resurfaced to a thundering of stones, his head and shoulders pelted with falling debris. A bigger fragment got him between the shoulder blades, making him grunt in pain. The flashlights faded. Jacob wiped his eyes and could still barely see for the dust.

He had moved away from the intersection down one of the other passages, and found it all but blocked by a serious cave-in. A stone the size of an armchair had fallen not two feet from him. The water frothed from its displacement.

Jacob whirled around to face the intersection again, and saw the lights of the two flashlights rapidly dwindling. A woman screamed. The rumbling waned, and it its place came a disturbing sound of crackling all along the ceiling.

"Is he dead?" one of the terrorists shouted.

"Whether he is or he isn't, let's get out of here," another shouted from the opposite corridor.

"I'll meet you at the ramp. Keep your eyes open."

The lights receded in both directions.

Jacob hesitated, looking first down one corridor, then the other. Save the German archaeologist or Jana?

Jana. She's Aaron's daughter.

Jacob felt something twist inside. He was making a choice between two lives based on personal preference. A horrible thing to do, and he hated himself for doing it. But he had to choose somehow.

He slid through down the corridor like a water moccasin pursuing its prey. Only his head and gun remained above water. Jacob worried about the gun. While modern firearms were generally waterproof, they had limits, and he worried about it jamming thanks to all the grit swirling around in the water.

Jacob pumped along with his feet, half swimming, half pushing himself along. The crackling from the roof continued. The woman shouted in German, the plaintive cry sounding like a banshee in the dim catacombs.

He began to gain on the terrorist holding Jana. The man's flashlight bobbed back and forth as he tried to wade through the water, pushing

Jana ahead of him, a gun to her head. As far as Jacob could tell, he didn't look back.

They were almost to the corner leading to the next passageway that ran to the landing. Apparently the other terrorist knew a way to loop around and get there. They must have grilled Inge Weber about the layout of this place.

But why the hell were they here? And why did they want her to read some ancient inscription?

He'd ponder that later. First, he needed to get Jana away from that guy before he killed her. But how could he catch up to them without alerting the terrorist to his presence?

Jana provided the answer by suddenly ducking low, spinning around, and punching him.

While Jacob couldn't see well, the man's falsetto shriek gave him a hint of where Jana's fist had landed.

Jacob felt almost as surprised as the unmanned terrorist. He rushed forward as fast as the tugging water would allow. The light jiggled crazily as the terrorist fought with Jana. The gun went off and Jana fell.

"You bastard!" Jacob shouted, hurling himself at him.

He hit him full force, both men toppling over Jana's body. Jacob hadn't shot for fear that Jana might still be alive, plus he wanted to kill this scumbag with his bare hands.

They plunged underwater. Jacob groped around until he found the Arab's gun hand. He grasped it with both of his and twisted. The man's beefy wrist didn't snap, but the pain was enough for him to drop his weapon.

Jacob felt the man's other hand grasp his ear, then work along his face to press at his eyes.

He rolled, shoving the man's hand away before he got blinded, and pushed them both above the surface to slam him against the wall.

That barely winded him, and Jacob got a right hook to the side of the head that made him see stars. For a second he could do nothing. A strong punch knocked him back down into the water. Hands groped for him, searching him out as Jacob struggled, sputtering as a bit of water got into his lungs.

His hand settled on a stone.

The terrorist grabbed him by the shirt front and shoved him downwards, trying to pin him underwater. Jacob's lungs protested. He felt like throwing up. His mind swirled. With the last of his strength, he struggled free, shirt tearing, then rose up and smacked the stone down on the top of the man's head.

It was a blind swing, and a weak one, but enough to make the guy let go. Sputtering and coughing, Jacob wiped his eyes and looked.

Just in time to see the Arab pull out a second gun.

Jacob slammed the rock down on him as hard as he could. He heard a sharp crack as the man's skull split and he fell straight down into the water.

Still coughing, Jacob staggered back and leaned against the wall for support. Movement nearby made him turn and raise his rock for another strike.

Jana stood there, wavering back and forth.

"You all right?" he gasped, still coughing up water.

"Yeah. Why the hell didn't you go after Inge?"

"I was saving you."

"I can take care of myself. Let's get going!"

"Yes, ma'am," Jacob grumbled. He reached for the terrorist's flashlight, visible only as a glow beneath the surface. The operatives of The Sword of the Righteous had come better prepared than they had, investing in waterproof flashlights.

Jacob plucked it out of the water and used it to find a pistol in the murky depths. Jana grabbed another one.

"Come on, let's move it!" she ordered, splashing through the water in the direction of the landing. Jacob hurried to keep up.

"How did you survive that burst of fire?" he managed to sputter out.

"I hid in one of the grave niches."

"You're full of surprises."

"And you're full of disappointments. You should have saved Inge."

Well excuse the hell out of me.

Jana rushed ahead. Jacob had to hurry to keep up. They were halfway to the landing before Jacob grabbed her shoulder and pulled her back.

"Watch it. You want to get killed? That won't help your friend."

He switched off the flashlight. The hallway continued straight, so they didn't need it to move forward.

Now that they stood in darkness, they could see a faint light ahead, growing brighter.

"They're approaching the landing," Jacob whispered. "Let's go."

They forged ahead, trying not to make too much noise. Inge's shouts and the Arab's curses helped muffle the sound of their movements.

A light appeared ahead, the landing coming into clear view. The terrorist pushed Professor Weber ahead of him, his gun to the back of her head. A moment later they passed from view, headed up the ramp. Jacob and Jana picked up speed.

By the time they got to the landing, they could see the light was already more than a floor above them. The sound of running footsteps echoed down to them. They gave chase up the ramp.

The baleful glare of a flashlight appeared over the wall above them. Jacob pulled Jana back. The terrorist fired, the bullet cracking off the ramp just where Jana had been standing.

Jacob fired back, but the terrorist had already ducked out of sight.

They huffed up the ramp after him, keeping to the wall next to the chamber openings to stay out of the line of fire. Once Jacob leaned out to dare a shot, but only caught a glimpse of them, well above them now, going around the bend. The terrorist kept out of the line of sight too.

These guys might be willing to die from their cause, but they'd rather complete the mission.

He'd seen this before with The Sword of the Righteous. They weren't like a lot of groups. ISIS, Islamic Jihad, Al-Qaeda—those guys all had a death wish. They yearned to become martyrs and that affected their tactical thinking. The Sword of the Righteous reminded him more of the Taliban. The Taliban came from an age-old Afghani tribal fighting tradition with, for many of its members, just a thin overlay of Islamic fundamentalism. Mostly those guys wanted to be great warriors with martyrdom just a possible bonus. Looked like the fighters of The Sword of the Righteous felt the same.

As they got to the second level, the flashlight, plus the daylight streaming down from above vanished with a metallic clang. The guy had slammed the door shut. They heard the squeal of the rusty bolt snap into place.

By the time they got up there and smashed through, the terrorist, and his hostage, were long gone.

The look of hatred, of blame, that Jana gave him was the worst thing Jacob had experienced all day.

* * *

Ahmeen ibn Tariq, sergeant in The Sword of the Righteous, hid out in a palm grove a couple of kilometers from the ancient pagan tombs. The woman lay in a heap at his feet, sobbing and exhausted.

Weak. All Westerners were weak. Even the men. Some could fight like demons like that man back at the tombs, but their loose morals and erring religion made them weak. They would lose in the end, despite all their grand technology.

In fact, they would lose *because* of their grand technology.

Ahmeen ibn Tariq checked his phone. Yes, there was coverage out here. Not like in Syria, where most of the cell phone masts had been destroyed in the civil war.

He made a call. It got answered on the first ring.

"Report," demanded a severe voice.

"We've confirmed the writings."

"Good."

"Did you get the other package where it needs to be?"

"Yes. Join us at the rendezvous. Make sure you aren't followed."

"There's a problem. Someone else was at the tombs. A Western man with a woman. The man's a skilled killer. All the others have been martyred. Judging from the description, he's the same man who caused the trouble in Damascus a few days ago."

"Do you still have your package?"

Ahmeen ibn Tariq looked down at the woman at his feet, who looked up at him with wide, tear-rimmed eyes.

"Yes."

"Get rid of it, and then try and track down that man. Kill him and his companion or go to paradise trying."

"I will not fail, sir."

He hung up, then snapped the burner phone in two and tossed it into the grass.

The woman scrambled away a couple of feet before her back hit a tree and she stopped, trembling all over.

Ahmeen ibn Tariq studied her for a moment.

"It's a pity I don't have a video camera," he told her in German. "We have our own social networks, you know. Not like your TikTok or Snapchat. Not stupid people dancing to sinful songs. Real content. Sermons and acts of jihad. I'd get a lot of likes and shares for a video of you."

He drew a razor-sharp Bowie knife and approached her, smiling at the thought of committing another act that would help him gain paradise.

CHAPTER TWELVE

Jana slumped on her bed in the hotel they had gotten in Alexandria. She had run out of tears an hour ago, but the simmering anger against Jacob and the whole CIA remained.

The Company had taken her father and turned him into a distant figure she hardly ever saw, and then it had gotten him killed.

And now Jacob's shortsightedness had gotten Inge killed.

Deep down she knew that wasn't fair, that he had the chance to save only one of them and chose her, but she didn't care. The whole organization had hands dripping with blood. All their little games fighting foreign powers only ended up getting innocent people killed.

She had no doubt that Inge was dead, or soon would be. Jana had barely heard of The Sword of the Righteous, just another name among a flurry of similar groups that came and went with bewildering rapidity. But she knew the type. Bloodthirsty, driven, and full of hate.

Especially for an educated, successful Western woman like her friend. Or decent Muslims like Mohammed, the watchman at the catacombs.

I hope it was quick.

She shuddered and got up, pacing.

Jacob got them adjoining rooms in one of the old hotels that lined Alexandria's corniche. She had a big, airy room and a clean if somewhat antiquated bathroom. She moved to the French doors leading to the balcony and opened them, letting the warm sea breeze from the Mediterranean waft into her face.

The wide curve of Alexandria's shoreline spread out before her. Below, the seaside road was filled with honking traffic, and beyond that was a wide pedestrian boulevard filled with food vendors, laughing children, and Egyptian couples strolling and enjoying the last red traces of the sunset. Overhead, the first stars winked in an azure sky.

Beyond the pedestrian boulevard lay the broad stretch of Alexandria's harbor. Bobbing lights showed where a few fishing vessels and pleasure craft were moored or moving slowly across the water, and further on, the gray profile of an Egyptian naval vessel. The military was on high alert thanks to the tensions between the United

States and Iran. More posturing. More men wanting to show they were tough and not caring who got hurt in the process.

Like her father.

It's only for three weeks this time, honey, and then we'll spend all day at the zoo.

Three weeks. Three months. Who knew how long it would really be? Jana had counted the days, marking them off one by one on whatever boy band calendar adorned her room that year, the day of his return outlined in glitter.

And he'd almost always miss, come back late with a shamefaced apology about the work being tougher than he anticipated.

And Jana had always forgiven him, reveling in those great big hugs and being swung around and kissed like she was the most important little girl in the world.

The few precious days he'd be back would be a whirlwind of activities. The zoo, hiking, games in the park, the beach, her father giving her a wink and calling the school, "Yes, poor Jana's flu isn't getting better. She'll have to stay home another day." She would bask in attention and affection until the inevitable call came, and Dad's face went stony.

"Sorry, but duty isn't something we choose, it's something we carry. I hate to leave. I wish I could tell you what's going on, then maybe you'd understand."

"I understand, Daddy. We'll have twice as much fun next time!"

And she did understand, sort of. Her dad was an American hero, fighting the bad guys and protecting her and Grandma and Grandpa and the whole country. She thought he was some sort of military advisor, with hands free of blood. If she only knew.

Those absences still hurt, though, and each time it happened it would hurt more, and she'd go back dejected to Grandma and Grandpa's house, the only child of a dead mother and an absent father.

As that child grew, her acceptance dwindled. In her teens she'd act sullen during his increasingly rare visits, and at age twenty she gave him an ultimatum—be there for her twenty-first birthday or be gone. He texted her at the last minute, sending his regrets and his one millionth apology.

She hadn't spoken to him again. A year later two grim-faced operatives knocked on her door to tell her he was KIA. The government wouldn't even tell her where. His body was never returned.

Jana cursed and turned away from the beautiful sight of Alexandria's harbor. The CIA had taken her father, and then had gotten him killed.

She needed some air. Jacob had said to stay in the hotel but to hell with him. She could take care of herself. The Great Disappearing Daddy had made sure of that.

Turning off her lights to make it looked like she'd gone to sleep, she unlocked the door and eased it open and shut with barely a sound. The old-style lock rattled a bit, but in this echoing old building hopefully Jacob wouldn't realize the noise came from her room. Then she tiptoed to the old marble staircase with its cast iron bannister, a relic of the period a century ago when Alexandria was the center of a wealthy international community, and hurried downstairs.

Instantly she felt better. Walking along the boulevard, she breathed in the sea air and half-listened to the everyday conversations of the people around her. All those normal, decent people. No radical Islamists, no spies, no hired assassins. Just people.

The feeling of peace didn't last long. It never did.

Soon her mind turned back to the mystery of why a band of Sunni terrorists would want an Egyptologist to translate some obscure inscription in some little-known catacombs.

The discovery had made the press, of course, but she doubted more than a few dozen specialists had read the archaeological report that detailed the inscriptions and their translation. Certainly not the general public. Why in the world would The Sword of the Righteous take an interest in something like that, and go to the trouble of kidnapping Inge, bringing her all the way to Egypt, only to confirm what she had already published?

Like she had told Jacob, hieroglyphics were not her strong suit. She had hired Inge to do the translation because she was the best for the late period of Egyptian picture writing. Her translations about "the punishing power of Ra" had confused them both, and yet so many references in ancient religious writing were so obscure that they hadn't given it much thought.

Now she needed to. Jacob couldn't do this on his own.

Damn these people! You can never get away from them.

With a purposeful stride, she walked along the corniche for a mile to the east, until she came to the Library of Alexandria, the modern city's prize accomplishment. Meant to replace the famous ancient library, this avant-garde building with its curving concrete façade, engraved with dozens of languages and its vast reading room beneath sloping skylights, housed an impressive collection of books and ancient manuscripts.

More to the point, it had one of the world's best Egyptology collections.

It was closed at this hour, of course, at least to the general public.

She climbed the broad steps to approach the front door, where three guards lounged around sipping tea. She recognized the oldest one, a silver-haired man named Younis who had served in the military for many years before retiring to this easy job.

"Younis! So good to see you again."

After the traditional greetings and enquiries after family, Jana asked, "I need to look something up. Are any of the librarians still in the reading room?"

"Yes. Lillete is in there conducting some of her own research. I'm sure she'll let you work there for a while."

Younis let her through into an enormous main hall adorned with a larger-than-life portrait of the president, and she made her way to the reading room, multiple rows of desks taking up the size of two football fields. Lillete, a beautiful young Coptic woman who had already authored three history books, rushed up to her, all smiles.

The cheerful conversation usually would have buoyed her up, but Jana felt impatient, and only just managed to continue chatting long enough to remain polite. At last she sat at a desk, a pile of academic journals and field reports in front of her.

"Take all the time you need," Lillete said, squeezing her shoulder. "I have my own work to do and I was looking for an excuse to tell my husband."

Jana chuckled at that, and then got to work.

It took less time than she thought. While hieroglyphic studies was a vast field, it grew narrower in the period when the ancient language had to compete with that of its Greek and Roman occupiers. Also, excavations of those periods were less popular. The government tended to fund digs at older sites that were more likely to turn up gold statues and well-preserved mummies. Also, academics carefully indexed their translated texts. She narrowed it down further by only looking for texts referring to Ra and Sekhmet.

It didn't take long to find her first reference, a fragmentary inscription from the Greek period referring to the "punishing power of Ra." The discoverer noted that "this odd phrase is similar to an unclear passage in the passage of Berlin papyrus no. 694, excavated from a Greek period site near Luxor."

That reference number meant it was in the Berlin museum archives. She called over Lillete to get her the catalog that included that number, and within minutes read something that changed her perception of the problem entirely.

For the next hour she chased down three more references, and by the time she finished, sweat trickled down her back and her hands trembled.

It couldn't be right, and yet what other explanation is there?

She had to tell Jacob. This was far, far worse than she had ever imagined.

CHAPTER THIRTEEN

Jacob felt like an ass. He should have told Jana about her father earlier. Dragging her away from her excavation and into danger, he had an obligation to explain to her how good of a man Aaron Peters had been.

But he had chickened out. To explain would have been too awkward, too uncomfortable.

Because he would have had to explain too much.

He hadn't put two and two together until he had studied Jana's information in the dossier. Her date of birth, or more accurately her twenty-first birthday, coincided with the day her father had saved him.

Jacob had been a U.S. Army Ranger on a recon mission deep into Taliban territory, helping the pro-American government in Kabul fight a war Jacob had known all along it would lose.

They'd been hunting a high-ranking member of the Taliban on the run. It was just a few days into a major joint offensive when the top members of the Taliban had already headed to the hills, leaving the rank and file to get pummeled by airstrikes. Afghanistan's rugged terrain made the perfect hiding place, and the Rangers had so much ground to cover on those steep slopes and narrow valleys that they had divided up into platoons of thirty men each.

It was the only way they could have any chance of catching the guy, but it proved to be a tactical mistake. Because the local tribesmen, fiercely independent and many loyal to the Taliban, could pick off each platoon one by one, defeating the entire regiment in detail.

Masters of guerilla warfare, they hit two widely spaced platoons at the same time, making it harder for the Americans to support both.

Jacob's platoon was one of them.

The tribesmen attacked as they were going up a narrow ravine that led to a village they needed to check out.

The attack came without warning, and as a complete surprise since intel had told them this tribe was neutral. The crackle of small arms fire sounded from the cliffs above, echoing through the canyon. Some guy up there with a sniper's rifle took out the platoon commander with one shot, and two more guys fell shortly thereafter.

Everyone else hunkered behind rocks as the gunfire was strengthened by several rocket propelled grenades thumping down, splintering the rocky soil and sending fragments everywhere.

The platoon was already two-thirds of the way up the ravine, so the smart thing to do was to retreat forward, toward the village. A running fight, and two more wounded, got them there.

Like with so many valleys in Afghanistan, once you get through the ravine leading to it, you find yourself in a wide, circular depression of green grass and trees fed by countless mountain streams. The uplands were far enough away in each direction that Taliban small arms fire couldn't reach them, and the platoon stopped in a farmer's field in the dead center of the valley to bandage up the wounded and assess the situation.

A radio signal back to base brought the bad news that it was under heavy attack by a large Taliban force, as was another Ranger platoon. They couldn't expect any air support for at least an hour, since all available air cover was needed to help the base.

The Rangers decided to head for the village. While out of range of small arms fire, artillery and mortars could still hit them from the surrounding slopes, and their current position made them sitting ducks if the Taliban decided to bring in something heavier.

The village stood at the far end of the valley, clinging like a mountain goat to a steep slope and protected by a low wall that looked like it had been built in the Middle Ages.

Still, it would make a good defensive position. The Taliban in these parts were from the local tribe, and wouldn't fire on their own village.

Jacob and his platoon were greeted at the village entrance by a group of elders who, through their Afghani translator, assured them they wanted no trouble.

The peace lasted all of fifteen minutes.

Jacob was in a barn, treating a wounded comrade when it all kicked off. He heard the thump of a grenade, and several shots. When he rushed out, he found the platoon in chaos, shooting in every direction.

The firefight lasted only five minutes. A pair of teenaged kids, too young to grow beards but old enough in that culture to know how to fight, had decided to launch their own adolescent jihad and managed to kill a Ranger. Both teens died shortly thereafter, but that didn't end it.

The platoon snapped. Leaderless, hunted, exhausted from weeks of constant marching and fighting, they took out their rage on the villagers.

Jacob watched, paralyzed with horror, as men he'd fought alongside for months turned into animals. One tossed a grenade into a hut where some women were hiding. Another gunned down a small kid right in the middle of the street. Three more grabbed a young girl and started tearing her clothes off.

Jacob's whole world fell apart. He'd been raised a patriot, his deep love of country and the flag only strengthened by the camaraderie he'd found in the Army Rangers, an elite force whose conduct confirmed his conviction that they were on the side of right.

All that had been ruined. All of Jacob's beliefs got destroyed in an instant.

And that's when Jacob's mind broke.

He couldn't remember much after that, only vague images of gunning down the three men about to rape the girl, then taking out the guy, his best friend in the platoon, who had gunned down the kid.

Jacob shot a couple more before the platoon rallied and chased him off.

Jacob took to the hills, retreating straight through enemy lines and taking out of few of them on the way.

He had ended up in a cave two ridges away, with nothing but what he had in his pack, hunted by the Taliban, and hunted by his own side.

For months he lived like a shadow, sneaking out at night to raid farms for food, hiding in the daytime, killing anyone who came into his cave and shifting to a new one on a regular basis. This period, too, remained hazy in Jacob's memory, a nightmare of raging emotions punctuated by suicidal guilt. He became feral, living on his instincts, mistrusting the entire world.

Twice the U.S. military sent troops to find him, once a platoon from the Rangers, and the second time a Navy Seal team.

He had slaughtered them all to a man.

The third time they sent Aaron Peters. Alone.

From what Peters told him, he had located Jacob's cave after a long hunt and, curious, settled down to observe him over the course of a few days. The older man watched as Jacob—filthy, with matted hair and torn clothing—trapped rabbits and snuck into a nearby village to steal food. He watched as a Taliban patrol came dangerously close to his hideout and Jacob ambushed them, killing all five of them and stripping them of their blankets, food, and weapons.

And he watched as Jacob crept up on a lone shepherd boy. Convinced the madman was about to kill the youth, Aaron got him in the sights of his sniper's rifle, ready to take him out.

But all Jacob did was leap out from behind a rock and bellow like a Sasquatch on steroids. The boy yelped, dropped the antiquated musket he carried, and bolted for the nearest village. Jacob had already taken on an almost mythical status with the locals—half killer, half boogeyman.

Jacob proceeded to leap onto the nearest sheep and tear into its throat, drinking its blood and devouring its raw flesh.

Aaron shot him right through his center mass, his aim so expert he could avoid any major organs from a range of 500 yards.

"When I saw you spare that kid I knew you had some humanity left in you. I knew you could be saved," he explained months later.

Still, Aaron waited until Jacob had crawled more than a mile and passed out from blood loss before approaching him and patching him up.

"I wanted to save you, but not at the risk of my own life. Even wounded you were more dangerous than a dozen Taliban."

Aaron's orders were to exterminate Jacob, and bringing him back alive had nearly cost him his job. But the CIA agent pulled in several favors, got Jacob incarcerated in a secret mental institution, and made it his personal mission to rehabilitate him.

That healing journey, during which Aaron Peters eventually got him released, found innocent by reason of self-defense for killing his fellow Army Rangers, who were guilty of a war crime that got hushed up, was still far from finished.

A furious pounding on his door made him leap out of bed and draw the gun he had taken from the terrorist in the catacombs.

"Who's there?" he demanded, ducking into the bathroom to get out of the line of fire.

"It's me!" Jana said. "Let me in."

Jacob breathed a sigh of relief and unlocked the door.

"Where did you sneak off to? I checked your room a while ago and you were gone."

"I was at the library, looking up references to the 'punishing light of Ra.' I found that the catacombs and the Canopic jar we found there aren't the only mentions."

"Really? What else did you find?"

"Five other references. Three are just fragmentary and don't tell us much except that the term was more common than we thought. Then I found a papyrus from the Ptolemaic period that—"

"The what?"

"The Greek dynasty, or more accurately Macedonian dynasty, founded by Ptolemies. He was a general of Alexander the Great. When he died his empire got split up among his generals. Anyway, this papyrus was a fragment of a medical text, written in Greek by a physician in the first century BC. Check this out."

She held up her phone, showing a photo of some printed text in a book. It was all in Greek. Jana read it like she was reading a menu at a steakhouse.

"If the punishing light of Ra and Sekhmet escapes its container whether by design or happenstance, the invisible light will cause a number of symptoms. If the container is breached for only a moment, the patient may only suffer fatigue and a sick stomach. For longer, the patient will suffer the flux and fever. If the container is open for long, and the punishing light of Ra and Sekhmet is able to work into the patient, they will soon develop burns on their skin as if from being placed in the sun for days on end, and their hair will fall out. In the worse cases the patient will die. There is no cure for these maladies except to remove oneself from the punishing light as quickly as possible, and even then some ill effects are sure to follow."

Jacob stared at her for a moment. "It says that?"

Jana nodded.

"But ... that sounds like radiation poisoning."

"There's more. In another papyrus, from slightly later, there's this: 'The silvery metal stones of Sekhmet contain the punishing invisible light. Only after great rituals may the light be unleashed.'"

"That sounds like uranium! But naturally occurring uranium isn't radioactive enough to cause radiation poisoning."

"Isn't uranium radioactive?"

"Uranium 235 is the one used in bombs and reactors. It does occur naturally, locked in with uranium 238, which is way less radioactive and can't sustain a nuclear chain reaction. You have to refine it to extract the uranium 235."

"Could they have refined it somehow?"

"What? Into uranium 235? That's impossible. That didn't happen until the 20th century."

"Then how to explain these ancient texts?"

"I ... can't," Jacob admitted.

He thought for a minute. While he was hardly an expert, he knew that refining natural uranium to extract and concentrate the uranium 235 was a complex and highly technological process, and first you'd have to know that radiation existed in the first place. Could the ancient

Egyptians have known all that? Or maybe they came across a concentration of uranium that was naturally more refined?

"Damn," he gasped. "Do you think all that stuff about advanced ancient civilizations could be true?"

Jana rolled her eyes. "You've been watching too many bogus TV documentaries."

"But if they had uranium 235 they——"

"And if you mention ancient aliens I'll slap you."

Jacob snickered. "There are some classified Air Force reports I'd love to show you. Besides, you're the one talking about uranium 235 in Canopic jars."

Jana sighed, looking at her feet. "It's crazy, and yet it's the only answer I can think of."

"It sure explains why that Canopic jar was lined with lead, and it explains why The Sword of the Righteous is after it. Uranium is highly controlled. It's one of the few things the major powers agree on. Nobody wants it to get into the wrong hands. Even most arms smugglers will narc on someone trying to buy or transport uranium. A terrorist group with a nuke is bad for everybody."

"So they happened to read about my discovery, put two and two together, and went after some uranium no one can trace," Jana said.

Jacob nodded, his face turning grim and his stomach tying in knots. "And they could have a bomb any day now."

"They couldn't make one that quick, could they?"

"Professor Meyer isn't the first nuclear physicist to get kidnapped. One was abducted from Romania a couple of years ago. He worked at a nuclear power plant. Got snatched on his way home from work. No one ever saw him again. I guess he resisted or died or something, and they needed to Meyer to finish the job."

"Could some terrorist group really build a nuke?"

Jacob shrugged. "It's 1940s technology. With one decent nuclear physicist, and a few university-educated helpers, it wouldn't be much of a challenge. The real problem is getting the nuclear physicist and the uranium."

"And they have both."

"I need to make a call," Jacob said, moving to the closet where he kept his secure satellite phone.

CHAPTER FOURTEEN

Professor Klaus Meyer woke up groggy and cramped. The last day and a half had been torture. After the terrorists had bundled him into the van, he had been taken to a farmhouse in the German countryside. There, he had been put in a room separate from the Egyptologist. They hadn't hurt him; in fact they had made sure he was comfortable. They fed him regularly, asked him if he was taking any medications they could fetch for him, even asked if he had any food allergies.

This solicitous treatment only confirmed what he feared—that they wanted to use him to make some sort of nuclear device. Probably a dirty bomb. Uranium 235 was all but impossible to buy on the black market, but getting other radioactive material—waste from a power plant, for example—was easier. The International Atomic Energy Agency had long been worried about it. A conventional bomb packed with radioactive material could spread radiation over an area of several city blocks. Place it in downtown Manhattan or next to Buckingham Palace, and the result would be disastrous.

But he wouldn't make such a bomb for them. He'd rather die first. Meyer could only hope that he'd have the courage to say no when these barbarians set him in front of a video camera and put a knife to his throat.

He remained in that farmhouse all that day. He heard the woman only once, when they passed outside his locked door with her. She pleaded and sobbed. They only laughed. Shortly thereafter, he heard the van pull away.

After the sun set, his kidnappers came for him.

"Take these pills," one commanded, holding out a pair of little white tablets.

"W-what are they?"

"They will not hurt you. They're sleeping pills."

Meyer took them, wishing they were cyanide.

He had fallen into a deep slumber shortly thereafter, and the next thing he knew he was waking up, bound hand and foot, in the back of a different van than the one they had kidnapped him with. The back was sealed off, and he could see nothing but four blank metal walls and an Arab guard he hadn't seen before.

"Where are you taking me?" he asked.

The man replied in Arabic.

"I don't speak your language," Meyer said, switching to English, the only other language he knew. "Do you speak English?"

The man clicked his tongue and jerked his head backwards. Then he pulled out a strip of cloth and gagged him.

After a long, bumpy ride, the van stopped and the back door opened. Bright sunlight of a kind you never get in Germany pierced his eyes. The guard and three more men, only one of whom he recognized, pulled him out. As they took off his leg restraints he looked around to see barren, rocky desert all around him, the only features some low, rocky hills in the distance.

His captors led him to a collection of concrete buildings surrounded by a concrete wall topped with razor wire. A man with a Kalashnikov stood atop one of the buildings, looking out into the vastness of the desert. The van drove off down a dusty road as a metal gate opened for them.

Waiting inside for him were three well-dressed young men. One held a notebook. They looked like graduate students.

"We are honored to meet you, Professor Meyer," one of them said in English. "We've studied your career and are very happy to have you as the new leader to our team. You may call me Ahmed. I study physics. This is Omar, who studies metallurgy and engineering, and this is Hamza, who studies chemistry. I think we will work well together."

Meyer wondered what happened to the old leader of their team, but knew better than to ask.

Once the gate closed behind him with a loud clang, the guards took off his hand restraints.

"You must be tired after your long journey," Ahmed said, still acting the polite host. Omar handed him a bottle of mineral water and a power bar. "Let's show you our workspace and then we'll eat a proper meal. I'm afraid we'll have to speak in English. Omar speaks German, if you're missing your native language, but unfortunately the only other language we all have in common is English."

They led him to the largest building, which had no windows. A guard posted at the heavy steel door opened it for them. Another guard accompanied them inside.

When they stepped through, Professor Meyer stopped and gasped.

70

It was a fully stocked atomic laboratory. On a table to one side, as he feared, sat a metal case with a panel open on one side. In it he could see various wires and a detonator. There was no explosive, however.

"Impressive, isn't it?" Ahmed said with obvious pride. "It took years to construct. Working at a big Western university you can practically snap your fingers and get all this equipment, but the infidels deny us such things. You have already noticed the bomb. Your predecessor did a good job constructing it, but unfortunately refused to complete the final step. I hope you won't be so stubborn."

They led him to a nuclear-shielded isolation chamber, something referred to by Meyer and his colleagues as a glove box. A lead-lined box was fitted with a window made of leaded glass and two pairs of heavy black, radiation-proof gloves, sealed at the end, sticking through so researchers could manipulate the box's contents.

Ahmed grinned. "We must take the first step right away. We've been waiting for so long that we must put off lunch for a little longer. I apologize for our lack of hospitality, but this really is such an important moment for us. As a scientist, I'm sure you understand."

They led him to the glove box. When he saw was lay inside, Meyer again stopped short.

"Isn't that an ancient Egyptian artifact? One of those things they put the internal organs in?"

"It's called a Canopic jar. The pagans used them as part of their filthy rituals, thinking it would help them live forever. They must have had quite a nasty surprise when they ended up in the place of painful chastisement." Ahmed and the other two graduate students snickered.

"Why do you have it?"

"Because the Devil taught them much, and we will turn evil into good. Please put your arms through the gloves. Since you are our team leader, we'll give you the honor of opening it."

Baffled, Professor Meyer stuck his arms into the radiation-proof gloves all the way up to his shoulders. While thick, protective material made fine manipulation difficult, he had years of experience.

The Canopic jar was clamped to the base of the isolation chamber. A mallet and chisel lay next to it.

Omar put his arms through the second set of gloves.

"Please break open the top," he said. "It's alabaster but the inside is lined with lead, so you'll have to put some muscle into it."

The cap had a lion's head on it. Confused, Professor Meyer picked up the mallet and chisel and placed the edge of the chisel where the cap met the body of the jar.

While no antiquarian, Meyer didn't want to break an ancient artifact.

"Yallah!" the guard snapped, making the professor cringe.

"That means hurry up," Omar said. "I'd do that if I were you. He's one of the rough ones."

Sweat beading on his brow, Meyer smacked the end of the chisel with the mallet. A tiny crack appeared at the seam.

"Harder," Omar said.

He hit it again. The crack widened.

"Come on, professor. Harder!"

Meyer gave it a good smack. The rim of the cap shattered and the lion's head rolled away. The Geiger counter fitted inside the isolation chamber clicked, its needle showing a trace amount of radiation.

Sweeping away the fragments, he found the opening to the Canopic jar sealed with lead.

"Now chip away that," Omar said, breathless with excitement.

Meyer did as he was told, making little chips around the rim, the tip of the chisel easily piercing the soft metal. As he did, the Geiger counter crackled louder and louder, its needle moving up.

Once he worked all the way around, the lead seal fell out. The Geiger counter now showed lethal amounts of radiation. If it wasn't for the isolation chamber, they'd all start feeling sick within the hour.

Omar took over, unclamping the jar from the base of the isolation chamber and turning the jar upside down.

That's when Professor Meyer got the shock of his life, because falling out of it came a disk of dull grayish metal.

Everyone took in a sharp breath.

"That's … but that's … " Professor Meyer couldn't finish, because he couldn't believe his eyes.

"Uranium 235," Ahmed said, his voice almost stilled with awe. "Gathered by the ancients. An Egyptian professor who used to study the pagans before embracing the true path told us of this. He doesn't know if it occurred naturally or they had discovered the secrets of refinement. It doesn't matter. It was theirs, and now it's ours. From the hands of the pagans, Allah has delivered it to the true believers."

Meyer pulled his arms out of the gloves. Wiping his brow, he tried to speak, but his voice came out in a squeak. He cleared his throat, put his shoulders back, and said, "I'm not going to make a bomb for you. And don't threaten me with torture because it won't work. I know you'll kill me in the end anyway. I'd rather die with my conscience clean."

The terrorists stared at him a moment. Omar yanked his arms out of the gloves with a snap. He glared at the nuclear physicist and reached into his pocket.

Meyer took a step back.

I hope it's quick.

But Omar didn't pull out a weapon. He pulled out a phone. He brought up the gallery and showed it to Meyer.

It was a photo of his wife, taken from a distance as she bought meat at the local butcher's. Meyer gulped. Omar swiped, and another photo appeared of her entering their house. Another swipe, and a photo of his teenage sons appeared as they played football in the park.

"No. Oh, no," Meyer moaned.

Omar kept swiping, showing photos of his brother and sister-in-law, and their little girl. Then came a photo of the retirement home where his father lived, and then another photo from Austria showing his sister.

"You will help us," Omar said, "or all these people will die in the most painful, humiliating ways our operatives can imagine. And believe me, they are quite imaginative."

Meyer stared at the phone, stunned to silence.

"Give us your answer," Omar said.

Meyer couldn't find the strength to speak. Ahmed stepped forward and slapped him hard across the face.

"Answer!"

Meyer bolted for the door. He didn't make it more than three steps before the guard drove a fist into his stomach, dropping him to his knees, doubled over in pain.

"Answer! If you don't answer right away, we start killing. We'll start with your two boys."

Sobbing, pounding his fist on the floor, Meyer shouted, "All right, you animals, all right! I'll do it."

"And don't try any tricks like making it a dud," Ahmed said. "While we need your help, we know enough to tell if you're doing it right or not. Any delays, any hint of deception, and the heads of your two boys will be floating in that lake where they play with their model sailboats. Next comes your wife."

Struggling to catch his breath, Meyer gasped, "All right. I'll help you. God forgive me, but I'll help you."

CHAPTER FIFTEEN

Early the next morning, Jana was awoken by a soft sound by her door.

She jerked awake and leapt out of bed in an instant. To her surprise, she didn't see any intruder entering her room. Instead, she saw a slip of paper sticking below the door, a pale rectangle of white in the shadows.

Jana tiptoed over and picked it up. She heard no noises in the hall. Whoever had put the note there knew how to move silently.

Just like she did.

She picked up the note and had to hold it up to the dim predawn light filtering through her window in order to make out the words.

"Jana,

"I'm sorry I pulled you into this and for not being honest about your father. Thank you for your help. You advanced the mission a great deal. Your father would have been proud.

"I need to go now. The mission is going to take me to another country and in more danger that I can honorably expose you to. You'll find the Company has put some money in your bank account for services rendered. Good luck on your excavation."

"Jacob"

Dad would have been proud? Would he have been proud of me letting Inge's murderers get away?

Jacob will kill them, if he can.

"If you want a job done right," Dad always used to say, *"You better do it yourself."*

She unlocked her door as quietly as possible and eased it open just in time to see Jacob slipping out of his room and tiptoeing down the darkened hall, a bag slung over his shoulder.

Jana moved to follow, keeping to side of the hallway where the shadows were deepest.

The long hallway was lined with doors under which no light shone. At the end of the hallway was a small lounge and reception. A hotel employee would be there, Jana knew, although at this hour they may well be asleep.

Jana trailed him for all of five seconds before Jacob whirled around.

She could have sworn she hadn't made any noise, and yet he had obviously heard her.

His hand reached under his shirt, where Jana guessed his gun to be hidden. Jana jerked back and raised her hands.

At that moment, Jacob recognized her. His body relaxed, he shook his head, and we walked back to her, silent as a ghost.

"What the hell do you think you're doing?" he whispered.

"Seeing where you're going," she whispered back.

He gestured at her. "Like that?"

It was at that moment that she realized she was still only wearing her underwear and halter top.

"I didn't have time to change," she said, hoping he couldn't see her blush.

"Let's go back to your room. I don't want anyone spotting us like this."

They tiptoed back down the hall and to her room, where she closed the door.

"If the guy at reception catches us he'll be scandalized," Jacob said.

"Shut up and let me dress." She left the light off. He had seen enough already.

Jana put on her pants, then her socks and shoes.

"No need for those. You're not going anywhere," Jacob said.

"Like hell I'm not. I'm going where you're going. By the way, where are you going?"

"You didn't even want to be on this mission."

"That was before Inge got kidnapped."

Even in the half-light of the room, Jana could see him slump a little and look away.

"What?" she asked.

"I was going to have someone call you."

She stood up and walked over to him. "What?"

"Her body was found by a shepherd yesterday afternoon not far from the dig site."

For a second Jana simply stood here, the entire room distant, her insides hollowed out.

She sat down hard on a chair. She thought of Inge, and Inge's kind husband, an engineer. And their little girl who loved flowers and superheroes.

For some reason the tears didn't come. Grief had been put on hold. Only rage had room in her heart.

"They cut off her head, didn't they?" she heard herself say.

75

"It was quick. No evidence of torture or … assault."

"They cut off her head, didn't they? Because that's what these bastards do."

Jacob looked about to put a reassuring hand on her shoulder, then hesitated and pulled it away.

"I'm sorry," he said. "I'll get her justice. My superior believes our theory about the uranium 235, but it's hard for the higher-ups to swallow. He needs proof to get approval for a larger operation. Until then I'm on my own. I have an idea where to get that proof, a place in Lebanon. I can't tell you more except that it's too dangerous for you to go there."

"I want to go anyway," she said, looking up at him.

He shook his head. "Where I'm going, the only women you'd see are in chains."

"I have to avenge her."

"No. Don't go down that path. I've … been there. It doesn't bring justice and all it does is poison you. Go back to your dig. Live a decent life. I'm sorry I dragged you into this. Remember that you helped a lot, and if I neutralize The Sword of the Righteous, it's because of your help. I have to go now. Goodbye and good luck."

He walked softly out of the room and closed the door.

Jana sat there for only a couple of seconds, fuming. Then she stood and with a few deft movements, packed all her things. Dad had taught her the importance of keeping everything ready for a rapid departure.

Always have a bugout bag, he used to say, *even when you're comfortable at home.* Especially *when you're comfortable at home. And when you're traveling, don't spread everything around your hotel room. Keep everything packed that you're not using right that moment.*

Odd advice that she had never thought she'd need and yet had always followed.

Jana opened her door a crack. The corridor was silent and empty. She moved fast on quiet feet down to the end. As she suspected, the old man at reception had his head and arms resting on the desk, sound asleep.

She moved to the staircase, and hesitated.

Something told her she wasn't alone.

Jana moved to a more shadowy part of the stairwell—little light filtered in from the single small lamp in the hotel office—and stood listening.

She heard nothing, and yet she felt sure she wasn't alone.

Jana dared a peek over the railing. The stairwell lay swathed in shadow, the ground floor three stories down was brighter, the front door open to the street and allowing the predawn light and the streetlights to shine in while leaving the corners and the area behind the large wooden doors in shadow.

One of those shadows moved.

Jana tensed. Jacob wouldn't have been so obvious. Someone else was down there, waiting.

Waiting for them.

She set her bag down on the stairs, slowly unzipped it so as not to make even a hint of any noise, and pulled out a 9mm automatic pistol that she'd taken from the fight the day before. Jacob hadn't objected at the time. Later, in her hotel room, Jana had stripped it and let it dry out after it had gotten dunked in the water of the catacombs, and then reassembled it.

Dad may have been useless as a father, but was pretty good as a teacher. All those survival skills he had drilled into her were now coming in handy.

He hadn't taught her how to survive a potential terrorist ambush with only two rounds in the magazine, however. She'd just have to improvise that.

Jana slung her bag over her shoulder and eased the safety off, wincing as it made a soft click.

Hugging the far wall so as to remain unseen from anyone below, Jana began to make her way down, step by silent step.

A sound made her freeze. A scuffle, a clatter of something metal falling on stone, a soft strangled cry.

Then nothing.

Jana held her position to the count of ten, and when she heard nothing more, crept down the stairs, checking every corner, every shadow.

She found a dead man in the lobby, tucked in the shadow of the open door, his neck broken.

Jana peered at his face and thought she recognized one of the terrorists from the catacombs. She couldn't be sure; it was dark here and dark and confused there, but it would make sense.

If this is the same guy, this was the man who killed Inge.

She spat in his face, then searched him. No weapon.

Jacob must have taken it. Greedy bastard.

She peeked out the front door onto the quiet street running perpendicular to the seafront. No one in sight except for a couple of sleepy Egyptians strolling away from her, probably going to work.

Jana went out on onto the boulevard that paralleled the curve of Alexandria's harbor and spotted Jacob two blocks away getting into a cab.

She looked around for another cab and didn't see one.

"Damn it!"

Then she saw a middle-aged man in a cheap suit getting into a battered old Fiat not far away. She hurried over to him.

"I'll give you a hundred dollars if you follow that taxi," she said in Arabic.

The man, startled at being accosted by a Western woman, paused for a moment, then looked her up and down.

"A hundred dollars is all you get," she said. "Touch me and I'll break your hand."

"I have to get to work."

"A hundred and fifty."

"I didn't want to go to work anyway."

They got in and sped off after the rapidly dwindling taxi.

"Don't get too close," Jana said. "Hang back a bit. If you can get a car between you and the taxi, do it. But not a truck, because then we won't be able to see."

"This isn't going to get me in trouble, is it?"

"No," Jana said, a grim smile spreading across her face. "But it will get me in heaps of it."

CHAPTER SIXTEEN

Jacob recognized the pilot as soon as he got onto the private landing strip on the outskirts of Alexandria. Orhan Yildirim was a short, compact Turkish-American of indeterminate age, with a lean, wiry body that Jacob could tell was the result of a lot of time spent in the field. While Yildirim didn't work for the Company, he was a trusted gun-for-hire. He acted as a guide and fixer all over the eastern Mediterranean and also doubled as a pilot.

"Nice to see you again, Orhan," Jacob said, taking his hand in his. Orhan's grip was firm and his hand calloused, especially the trigger finger.

Orhan flashed him a grin, bright in the rising sun. "Beirut this time, eh? What's the cover story?"

"Private businessman coming in for a bank deal. I'll change into a suit on the plane. Which one is it?"

"This way."

Orhan led him across the tarmac, where several planes were parked.

When Jacob saw that they were headed for a six-seater Cessna, he asked, "That doesn't have the range to get us to Beirut, does it?"

"This is the 210 Centurion. It's got a range of 1,000 miles. The best of the mid-sized Cessnas. That's why I use it. Dump your stuff in there."

Jacob threw his bag in the middle row.

"We're all fueled up and ready to go, but I need you to help me haul something into the cargo hold."

"All right."

They went into a nearby hanger, where a mechanic working on another plane took one look at them and left. Yildirim led him to a large metal cage of thick steel mesh, used a key to remove a heavy padlock, and gestured to a metal footlocker sitting on the bottom. Several other crates and boxes took up the rest of the space. Jacob knew better than to ask.

Whatever Yildirim planned to smuggle into Lebanon, it was heavy as hell. Jacob gripped one end while the Yildirim held the other, and together they sweated and strained their way to the plane.

"Don't give me a hernia, Orhan, I've got an important mission."

"Wuss."

Once they had stowed the crate, they climbed aboard and put on headsets that would both dampen the noise of the uninsulated engine and allow them to speak to each other via an internal radio.

With an expert's combination of ease and care, Orhan Yildirim went through the preflight procedure, then taxied down the runway, talking with the air traffic controller. They waited as a cargo plane took off, then got into position and took off a safe distance after it.

Jacob let out a breath of relief to be leaving the first part of the mission behind him, and to be leaving Jana too. That woman made him feel both guilty and nervous. He hated bringing civilians along on missions.

Yildirim didn't count. While he didn't work for any agency, he was anything but a civilian.

The plane headed out over the waters of the Mediterranean, golden in the rising sun, then turned northeast toward Lebanon. To their right stretched the green of the Nile Delta, to their left nothing but water, and ahead the bright sunrise.

Jacob settled into his seat and relaxed. That guy lurking at the ground floor to the hotel was taken care of, and as far as he knew that was the last terrorist who they had fought in the catacombs. Plus he was probably the one who had killed the German Egyptologist. He wished he'd had time to dispose of the body, but lying where it was, Jana was sure to be woken up by the hubbub when it got discovered. Maybe she'd see it, recognize the guy, and know her friend had been avenged.

The important thing was that she was safe now. He'd gotten in touch with a local operative to keep an eye on her and make sure she got onto the next plane to Morocco.

And as far as vengeance went, that was just beginning.

He knew a place in Beirut where any bit of information could be gleaned for the right price. With a bit of luck, he'd get something solid on The Sword of the Righteous and their plans by tonight, and call back to his bosses so they'd be able to make a plan of action.

He wondered about the Romanian nuclear physicist who had disappeared a couple of years before. If Jacob's hunch was correct and he'd been kidnapped by the same terrorist group, that gave them plenty of time to build a bomb. They might have everything assembled and were just waiting for the uranium 235.

Damn, we have to hurry. The question is, where are they building it, and what's their target?

He didn't even wonder what happened to the Romanian. Killed trying to escape, or killed for finally refusing to work more, or killed when they discovered he had made the bomb faulty.

Whatever the Romanian had done to arouse their ire, he was a dead man now. That's why they'd gone after Meyer.

With these thoughts, Jacob fell asleep. The soldier's training had never left him. Get your rest when you can, because you never knew when you'd get it next.

His sleep was nothing but blackness. He hadn't remembered his dreams for years. For that, he felt profoundly grateful.

Yildirim's voice woke him up some time later.

"We'll see the Lebanon coast in an hour."

Jacob was awake and alert the instant he opened his eyes.

"I better change character," he replied.

He took off his seatbelt and clambered into the middle row, where he had a tailor-made suit the local operative had sent over. Unzipping the suit from its bag and laying it out on one of the seats, Jacob sat in the adjoining seat and began to undress.

Just as he pulled his shirt off, a movement between the two back seats caught his eye.

His hand snaked into his bag and came out with a pistol.

"Put your hands up and show yourself!" he demanded in Arabic.

He got the surprise of his life when the stowaway turned out not to be some terrorist, but Jana Peters.

"Who the hell is that?" Yildirim asked, looking over his shoulder. He'd drawn a gun too. Jacob hadn't even noticed he was carrying. Hiding anything from his trained eye was quite a feat.

"This is a very persistent and extremely annoying civilian," Jacob growled.

"Well, dump her out the door. No one stows away on my plane and lives."

"Take it easy, Orhan." He turned back to Jana. "What the hell do you think you're doing?"

"Coming with you. What does it look like?"

"This isn't any of your concern."

"A terrorist group kills my friend and wants to start World War III and you're saying it's none of my business?"

"Too much information!" the pilot said. He worked on a strictly need-to-know basis and preferred it that way. In this line of work, ignorance was often bliss.

"You can't come with me." Suddenly Jacob realized the situation. "Wait. How the hell did you get this far?"

"I followed you out of the hotel and got someone to tail you. That was the worst part. The idiot practically drove up your exhaust pipe. No idea how to tail someone."

"I saw him. I thought he was just a bad driver. There are so many in Egypt. He backed off after a while and I lost sight of him."

"Thanks to me," Jana snorted. "I had to teach him everything. Then I snuck into the airport and got into the plane while you two got whatever is in that giant footlocker in the back. Are they guns? We're going to need them."

"That footlocker is none of your damn business," Orhan growled. "Jacob, throw her out."

"How about I throw you out?" Jana snapped.

"And who the hell is gonna fly the plane? You, superspy?"

"Shut up, both of you," Jacob said. Orhan replied with a string of Turkish swear words.

Jacob studied Jana for a moment, admiration overtaking exasperation. "Where did you learn to tail people like that?"

"My deadbeat dad. On the rare occasions I actually got to see him, he taught me all sorts of skills I never thought I'd need."

"You fought pretty well in the catacombs," Jacob admitted. "But I can't take you along. Beirut is a rough place."

"I know. I've been there."

"I'm not talking downtown where all the banks and hotels are. I'm talking northeast side. You been there?"

Jana paled. "No."

"You've heard of it, though. Right?"

"Yes."

"Then you know it's populated by militias, human traffickers, drug manufacturers, and mercenaries."

"And some really good bars," Orhan added.

"No place to take a lady," Jacob said.

"I'm not a lady."

Orhan looked over his shoulder, grinning. "Oh, really?"

"Shut up, whoever you are."

"I'm going to charge extra for this," the pilot grumbled, facing forward again.

"Look," Jacob said, trying to contain his impatience. "I can't take an untrained civilian along on a mission like this. It could get you killed. Hell, it could get me killed. Now that we're beyond the archaeological stuff, you're not an asset anymore. You're a liability."

"I'm not untrained."

Orhan snorted. "A few tips from Daddy ain't gonna cut it where he's going."

"Nobody asked you," Jana shot back. She turned to Jacob. "I'm coming, and that's it. You might still need my archaeological knowledge, and having a second set of eyes could prove useful. Now I know you're better trained than me. You can fight better than me. I understand that. But you need my help and you're going to get it, whether you like it or not."

Orhan whistled. "Wow, Jacob. She's a handful. You should stick to something a little fluffier."

Jana frowned at him. "Is he always like this?"

"Yeah," Jacob said, "but he's a good pilot. You do realize we could both die a gruesome death, don't you? And if you fall into their hands alive, you'll suffer a lot more than I will."

"Yes," Jana said, her voice wavering a bit. "But considering what's at stake, I'll take that chance. If they get what they want, we might all die anyway."

"Yeah," Jacob said and sighed. "You got a point there."

She had half convinced him. Jana really had proven useful so far, and there might be more archaeological questions coming up on this mission, since the whole thing was tied to one of her discoveries.

Plus he knew that ditching her in Beirut wouldn't get rid of her. She'd find a way to follow him. He couldn't do the mission and try to dodge her at the same time. Taking her along was a major headache, and a major danger, but if she was going to pursue this mission anyway, it would be far safer to have her where he could keep an eye on her.

Jacob finished dressing as the three of them settled into silence, each lost in their own thoughts. Jacob didn't know what was going through the heads of his companions, but he sure knew what occupied his own mind.

He was trying to figure out how to keep Jana alive in the darkest hole of the entire Middle East. Because if he wanted to discover some intel on The Sword of the Righteous and their plans for nuclear holocaust, that's where he'd have to go.

And taking a woman along would make it twice as dangerous.

CHAPTER SEVENTEEN

An hour later, after clearing customs with his tale of being a visiting businessman with his "companion"—a statement that got chuckles from the Lebanese official and a glare from Jana—Jacob emerged from the airport with his unwelcome guest to find a taxi waiting.

He recognized it as the right one because it had the logo of Homenetmen Sports Association Beirut emblazoned on the side. He'd never heard of that football team and had only memorized the logo because Tyler Wallace had sent him the information that this was the signal for the local operative.

A bit of research had told Jacob that Homenetmen S.A. was in the fourth division, perpetual losers in a sport where Arab pride mingled with fanboy enthusiasm. Nobody followed that team and so it made a good signal marker. It wasn't like any other cabbie would have their logo on the side of his taxi.

Even so, he studied the cabbie's face before he got in. Yes, it was the same man in the photo, a middle-aged Lebanese with curly black hair going gray and a belly that in a non-Muslim would have been developed through years of drinking beer. In his case, the culprit was more likely an affection for Lebanon's deliciously gooey sweets.

Jacob and Jana got in the back, keeping their luggage with them. Again Jacob couldn't help but feel impressed. A civilian would ask to put their bag in the trunk. Operatives kept their bags close to them at all times in case they needed to run.

A small detail, but a telling one.

The driver headed north along the seaside highway. Several ultramodern buildings of glass and steel—luxury apartments and offices for the nation's wealthy—clustered along the shore. Further back stood poorer, uglier buildings of concrete, their rooftops littered with washing lines and rusty satellite dishes. Heavy traffic tied up the highway, and the driver had to weave between slower vehicles.

"I suppose you had to ditch your weapons on the plane," the driver said in perfect English. Jacob detected a slight Australian drawl. He didn't ask how he got it.

"Yeah," Jacob replied.

The driver patted a sports bag in the passenger's seat. "Everything you need is in here. It's already got a label on it with your fake name. We got you two adjoining rooms in a nice little hotel downtown. The place is clean. No bugs of either kind. Owned by an Armenian family that doesn't belong to any faction. You're safe there as long as you keep up the façade. If you need anything more, you know how to contact me."

"I could use some backup," Jacob said, giving Jana a sidelong look.

"Afraid not. Hezbollah looks like they're about to start a major campaign of launching missiles into Israel and all boots on the ground need to be on that. If you weren't so high priority you'd be riding in a real taxi. I got to head to the border as soon as I drop you off."

"Understood," Jacob grumbled. As much funding as the CIA got, the chaos of the world always kept its personnel overstretched.

"I'll try to send a warning just before it kicks off. You don't want to be on the street when Hezbollah starts one of their rallies." The cabbie gave Jana a significant look in the rearview mirror.

Yeah, yeah. I know she's a liability. But you don't know how hard this woman is to shake.

The hotel was an old Ottoman mansion with windows screened by elaborate wooden latticework and a central courtyard shaded with a fragrant orange tree. As they stopped in front, a group of teenage boys laughed at the logo and aped fumbling an imaginary football. The cabbie blushed. Jacob and Jana were greeted at the door by a thin, swarthy man wearing an old-fashioned suit and an apologetic air.

"There's no electricity at the moment, I'm afraid. The entire neighborhood is out. The utility company says we'll get it back this evening, but … " he gave a helpless shrug.

The taxi drove off to howls of teenage derision.

"I've been to Lebanon before," Jacob said.

"Then you know it's only getting worse," the hotel owner said, leading them upstairs.

It had been getting worse. The Lebanese government had racked up a huge foreign debt, and that combined with a crumbling infrastructure and a shortage of fuel thanks to the trouble in the Persian Gulf meant brownouts or blackouts across the nation. If Hezbollah launched missile strikes into Israel, they could rally discontents among Lebanon's large population of urban poor and cause a lot of trouble for the weakened government.

And they might do just that. Hezbollah followed the Shiite branch of Islam, as did about half of Lebanon's Muslims. They were supported by Iran and might take the trouble in the Gulf as an opportunity to expand their power here.

There had been a war between the Shiites and the Sunni in Lebanon before, and it had led to a decade of misery and destruction.

The rooms the Armenian gave them were cool and dark, with high ceilings and creaky old beds. Once he had made his departure, Jacob turned to the archaeologist.

"I need to get going."

"Not without me."

Jacob shook his head. "Too dangerous."

"We've had this conversation. I'm coming and that's that. You need backup, and that fake cabbie can't give you any."

Jacob snickered. "You got a lot of your father in you."

Jana glared at him. "I wouldn't know. I hardly got to see him."

"He talked about you a lot," he said, his voice softening.

"He never mentioned you at all."

"That's because he didn't meet me until after you cut him off."

"Really?" she looked surprised. "When I got his things after he … after he was killed in action, there were heaps of photos of you together. In some jungle, in the mountains, in a bar in what looks like Bangkok. All over. And judging from the different clothes and haircuts, you guys hung out for years."

"We did. He was a good man."

"That's what you think."

"That's what I know," Jacob snapped. He owed Aaron Peters everything—his job, his life, his soul.

Jana didn't reply.

"Look," Jacob went on. "I need to go to a bar on Beirut's northeast side. You know what that zip code is like. If you insist on coming along, you'll play it my way, all right?"

"All right," she said, looking serious.

"Now let's see what the cabbie left for us."

Jacob unzipped the sports bag and, underneath a couple of sets of football kit for Homenetmen S.A., he found two 9mm automatic pistols with a large supply of hollow point rounds, a MP5 submachine gun with a 40 round box magazine and spare ammo, two teargas grenades, and two stun grenades. There was also a rather thick fountain pen. Jacob opened it up and confirmed that it was a single-shot .22 pistol.

"Take one of the 9mm pistols, one each of the grenades, and I'll show you how to use this pen gun," Jacob told her. He studied the archaeologist for a minute. "You ever kill anybody?"

"No."

"Ever shot a gun in anger?"

"No."

"Still want to go on this job?"

A glint came to Jana's eye. "They cut my friend's head off, and if we don't stop them, they might set off a nuke. So yes, I'm all in."

Jacob nodded, impressed.

Yes, you do have a lot of your father in you. I just hope there's enough, because where we're going, we're going to need it.

CHAPTER EIGHTEEN

"The first thing you need to learn about undercover work is to keep your eyes open and your mouth shut," Jacob said as they walked down a teeming side street in Beirut's northeast side. His gaze darted in every direction, alert for any sign of danger

"Especially if I'm a silly little female sidekick in some manly escapade," Jana teased.

God, why am I saddled with her?

"Take it any way you want, but listen to my advice. If your eyes are open, tell me what you see."

The street was barely wide enough for two compact cars to pass each other, and filled with a honking, slow-moving mass of cars and motorcycles. The narrow sidewalks were all but blocked by street vendors hawking cheap Chinese imports to the disinterested throng. To either side rose crumbling concrete apartment blocks, where even in Lebanon's mild winter, people hung out the windows to catch a breath of air.

"I see a lot of things," Jana said, "but if you're asking about the most important detail, it's that no one is staring at the two obvious foreigners."

"And why is that?"

"Because to look at an unusual situation is to involve yourself in it, and getting involved is really unhealthy in the Middle East, especially in a neighborhood like this."

"Your dad teach you that?" Jacob asked, impressed.

"No, my fifteen years traveling in the region did," Jana snapped. "I learned a lot more on my own than I ever did from him. I'm more than just your buddy's daughter, thank you very much."

"All right. So when we get to this den of vipers, you keep an eye on my back, and let me do the talking. Any questions?"

"Yeah. If we don't get any intel here, what's the next step?"

"No idea," Jacob admitted.

They kept walking.

The alley leading to the basement bar came into view just ahead. At the entrance to the alley, an old man sat on a low stool behind a cardboard box with a small stack of cigarette packs atop it. These cigarette sellers could be seen all over the Middle East. Some were simply men past productive working age trying to make a few extra coins for their families. Some were government spies. Jacob knew for a fact that this guy was a lookout for the bar. His earpiece was all but invisible beneath his keffiyeh.

The guy didn't blink as a Westerner in a business suit and a woman in khaki work clothes passed right by him and entered the alley. Jacob caught only the faintest whisper, all but inaudible thanks to the street noise, as the lookout radioed ahead with the announcement of their arrival.

Not that it was an issue. Everyone was welcome to enter Hassan's basement bar. Leaving depended on community consensus.

The bar had no sign. It was simply a set of concrete steps on the left-hand wall a few yards into the alley, leading to a door of reinforced metal.

Jacob pushed it open and entered a secret world.

At first glance, the place didn't look like much. A poorly lit basement with a low ceiling and the smell of mold; it had about a dozen round tables with chairs around them. A few pillars of bare concrete held up a low roof. No windows. Of course.

A short wooden bar took up half of the back wall, with no beers on tap and nothing but a refrigerator behind it, plus a dusty shelf of liquor bottles that didn't look like they'd been touched since the French had run Lebanon as a colony.

People didn't come here to drink. They came here to make deals.

Still, you had to keep up appearances. Jacob walked up to the bar, glancing to his left and right. A couple of tables were in huddles of whispered conversation. At a couple more, people seemed more relaxed, either having finished a deal or waiting for someone. At a table in the far corner, a man with so many scars on his face that he looked like a jigsaw puzzle sat staring into space.

Jacob knew him. A drug smuggler who could get you any controlled substance known to man. He was the nexus of several networks and, despite the shabby jacket and torn jeans, was worth more than some Third World countries.

He knew a few of the others too—a trio of arms smugglers, a corporate spy, a pair of mercenaries. He'd seen all their dossiers. To those who recognized him, Jacob was a shady businessman who worked all sorts of angles. That made him fit right in.

All the conversations hushed for a split second as everyone saw a woman enter. These guys were nearly unflappable, but the sight of Jana strolling into Hassan's place was something even people like them hadn't seen before. A moment later the guys remembered to be inconspicuous and returned to their conversations.

At the bar, he looked at Hassan, the one-eyed bartender, who didn't bother wearing a patch over his empty socket and said, "Two Almaza beers please."

"You want glasses with that?"

"No, thanks."

The glasses here were actually plastic. No good as weapons. It was better to have a bottle in your hand. Obvious tactical decision. In fact, *everyone* had a bottle in their hand.

Jacob would bet that they all had at least two or three guns and knives hidden on their person, but like his Turkish pilot, they were too good at concealing them for even an ex-Ranger CIA agent to spot them.

He paid with a hundred dollar bill and didn't wait for change. Hassan didn't give change. Then Jacob surveyed the room, picking who he'd speak to first. That pair of arms dealers sitting in the corner seemed a good bet. He strolled over. Jana kept right behind him. He hooked an arm around hers and brought her alongside. He needed to be able to see her. Every pair of eyes in the room had already checked her out, wondering why a woman would be here.

"May I join you?" he asked.

The arms dealers—one Serbian, the other Tunisian, both people he'd dealt with before—glanced at him, studied Jana a moment longer, and then gave a curt nod.

There was only one free chair. Jacob took it, leaving Jana to stand. This was not a time for gentlemanly courtesy. Jana turned to get her back to the wall, a move that also allowed her to watch Jacob's back, and sipped her beer.

"How can we help you, Mr. Tyson?" the Serb asked.

Tyson was one of Jacob's many aliases.

"I'm looking to prepare the groundwork for a business deal with The Sword of the Righteous, and I need to know their current needs before I approach them with an offer. You know how they are."

One of the rules to this place was getting to the point quickly. Time is money, and these people's time was extremely valuable.

The Serb snorted. "Watch it, my friend. I heard they ripped off Sergei for a shipment of hand grenades."

"I'm on an exclusive contract these days," the Tunisian added. "I haven't dealt with them for more than a year."

"What did they want when you last had dealings with them?"

90

"They wanted precision optics. Sights for sniper's rifles, artillery spotting equipment, that sort of thing," the Tunisian said.

Interesting. The Sword of the Righteous wasn't like some of the other militias. They didn't try to stake a claim to territory and hold it in open battle. While the sniper's scopes were pretty standard gear, they had no use for artillery. So they must need the optics for other purposes.

Jacob glanced at the Serb, who gave a brief shrug.

"I had no direct dealings with them. From what I heard, just the standard stuff. Nothing out of the ordinary for an outfit like that."

"Thanks." He got up, slipping a hand into his pocket. Two fingers only. It didn't pay to make anyone jumpy at Hassan's. He pulled out two stacks of bills wrapped with elastic bands. A thousand for the Tunisian, five hundred for the Serb, who had less useful information.

He dropped them onto the table in front of them. The slap of money hitting wood was the most common sound in this place.

Jacob turned and surveyed the room a second time. Those three mercenaries hunched over their beers might be a decent bet. He'd only dealt with one of them, a French guy who used to be in the French Foreign Legion, but he recognized the American and the Lebanese from the wanted posters.

This place was like a who's who of the World's Most Wanted. The CIA had long discussed taking it out, but decided it was more useful as a nexus of intel.

He strolled up to them. "May I join you gentlemen?"

"If you want to sell her, talk to Gregori," the American said, indicating an oily little man at another table.

"She's not for sale," Jacob said, not looking to Jana to see her reaction. He didn't want to know.

"Rent?" the Frenchman asked, raising one eyebrow.

"Afraid not, fellas." Jacob sat. Jana made the bold move of pulling a spare seat from the adjoining table and sitting down. Jacob hoped that hadn't been reserved for a drug kingpin or elite assassin.

A flicker of worry from the three mercenaries. Jana had just made a rookie move. Now she seemed even more out of place than before.

Jacob ignored her and said, "I'm looking to lay the groundwork for some business with The Sword of the Righteous."

The American shrugged. "Don't know much about those guys."

The Lebanese said, "I'm Shiite."

That was all the explanation needed. If he fell into their hands, he'd get his head cut off.

The Frenchman glanced at his two friends, and when they said nothing more, leaned forward, putting his hands flat on the table. "What kind of information are you looking for?"

"What are their current military needs?"

"Standard terrorist group, although more organized than most. I trained some of their men in the Syrian desert for a while. Squad tactics, urban warfare, demolition, that sort of thing."

"Good pay?"

"Very. But they fired me without notice."

"That happens sometimes. Did they give a reason why?"

The door to Hassan's bar opened. Everyone glanced that direction. Jacob saw a burly man in a hoodie, his face half obscured. The watchman had let him through, though, so he wasn't police. Jacob turned back to the former legionnaire.

"They wanted to move location and it was too sensitive to bring me along," the Frenchman said.

"Did they mention where?"

"No, but I found out."

Pause. The Frenchman looked at him expectantly.

Jacob pulled out $500 and slapped it on the table. The Frenchman kept staring. Jacob pulled out another $500 and slapped that on the table too.

He had no idea if this intel would be useful, but he did know it would be as accurate as the Frenchman's information could make it. In this sort of world, people relied on reputation.

"They went to the Sinai."

"What part?"

The man from the French Foreign Legion opened his mouth to reply, but then looked past Jacob to something behind him. Before Jacob could turn to look, he felt a tap on his shoulder.

Then he did look, and nearly wet his pants.

Because standing behind him was Chingis Beshimov, a Kyrgyz killer-for-hire. It had been him who had just come into the bar. Now he had his hoodie pulled back to reveal a shaved head and a long, thin scar down one side of his face.

A scar Jacob gave him in a knife fight in Bishkek two years ago.

That could have been forgiven—business was business, after all, and no one took these things too personally—except that Chingis knew he was CIA.

The Kyrgyz glowered at him, looking for all the world like his namesake Genghis Khan, and then opened his mouth to say something.

Probably the worst thing he could say in a place like this.
Jacob Snow's true identity.

CHAPTER NINETEEN

Jacob grabbed his bottle and swung it to add a second scar to Chingis's extensive collection.

The Kyrgyz killer blocked the blow, kicked Jacob's chair from under him, making him fall on his ass on the bare concrete floor, and bellowed out,

"He's CIA!"

That's not what anyone in Hassan's bar wanted to hear, least of all Jacob Snow.

He leapt up from the floor, overturning the mercenaries' table as he did so. They were about to get into the fight anyway.

Everyone was about to get into the fight, and all on Chingis Beshimov's side.

As the three mercenaries tumbled off their chairs, Jacob swung a killer right hook at the Kyrgyz who had narced on him, only to get it blocked and feel a meaty fist smack full on in his face.

God damn, I'm going to look ugly for another week.

Jacob staggered back, drawing a pistol even as he struggled to regain his balance.

Chingis was faster, probably because he wasn't seeing stars and having blood pour out his nostrils like a twin Niagara Falls.

The stars in Jacob's eyes cleared up just in time for him to see the gaping black hole of a .357 Magnum that was about to suck him into eternal darkness.

The gun blared, but to his utter surprise, Jacob didn't die. Jana had swung up with her bottle and smashed it into Chingis's elbow. The bullet hit the ceiling and ricocheted somewhere. Jacob hoped it hit someone.

He aimed at the Kyrgyz killer and let off his own shot.

That missed too, because just as he pulled the trigger he got tackled by the American mercenary in a move that showed he had been the star of his college football team before deciding that war paid better than the NFL.

Jacob landed hard on his side, getting his left arm up in time to cushion his fall. He pistol-whipped the American, kicked him off, and aimed at Chingis again.

No shot. He was struggling with a female archaeologist who was doing a very good imitation of a polecat.

OK, Jacob realized the comparison might have been sexist, but it was technically accurate.

Jacob kicked the legs out from under the Lebanese mercenary, who was just coming up to him, knife in hand, kicked him again in the face as he fell to the floor, then leapt up, landing on his feet.

He rushed to help Jana, but got cut off by the Frenchman, a hulking fellow who knew his way around a fight. The guy came at Jacob with a broken bottle in one hand and a knife in the other.

Jacob ducked the knife, got a shallow cut along the forearm from the bottle and gave the legionnaire a punch that would have felled a normal man but only seemed to piss him off.

Again that double combo of the knife and the bottle, and again Jacob dodged the more dangerous weapon only to get nicked by the bottle.

This is ruining my suit, and may ruin my life.

Just then, he and the legionnaire got rudely interrupted by a pair of human traffickers rolling between them, their hands at each other's throats.

Jacob backed up and realized the entire room had exploded into violence. He had expected that, but expected it to be all directed at him. Instead, half a dozen fights raged in the small bar, and a couple of people were already lying in pools of their own blood.

It looked like everyone was taking the opportunity to settle old scores, or maybe they thought Jacob was only one man in a larger sting operation, and anyone who had the least suspicion attached to them was getting attacked.

Jacob had no time to dwell on that, because the legionnaire leapt over the two human traffickers in their death clutch and came at him.

Jacob was ready for him this time, and gave him a roundhouse kick that knocked him several feet to the side, and straight into another fight. Jacob ducked the other direction, looking to help Jana.

Only to find her already down, and Chingis coming at him, shouting a war cry in his own language.

By this time, the entire bar was in chaos. Bottles flew through the air. Tables flew through the air. *Men* flew through the air. The proprietor, Hassan, had taken the wise move of hiding behind the bar, which Jacob had heard was backed with bulletproof steel. All Jacob could see of him was the top of his head and the tip of a shotgun.

He had no doubt that shotgun would blast him to pieces if Hassan got a clear line of fire.

And he also had no doubt that Hassan was a crack shot, so his best short-term survival strategy was to close with a murderously enraged descendant of Genghis Khan.

At least Chingis didn't clutch that hand cannon anymore. Jana must have disarmed him. Jacob hoped she wasn't too badly hurt. She was turning out to be more useful than he thought. Maybe he'd keep her around if they both survived the next five seconds.

Jacob smacked the heel of his palm into the charging Kyrgyz and swept his foot under his legs to knock him to the floor.

At least that's what he intended on doing. He connected with his hand, but his foot missed and suddenly he found he wasn't making contact with the floor anymore.

Instead he was flying through the air, and the next thing he made contact with was a concrete pillar.

The breath whooshed out of his lungs and he landed on the floor with an audible thud.

While Jacob would have preferred to lie there for a good hour or two recovering, a huge Kyrgyz foot was flying for his face and he decided he probably should do something about that sooner rather than later.

All he was capable of was to topple to one side, something he had been tempted to do to begin with.

Chingis's foot missed him by an inch, enough to save his skull, but too close to save his olfactory glands. The guy needed some foot powder.

Jacob ended up lying on the floor. Chingis staggered from the pain of kicking a pillar, then, snarling, tried to stomp on Jacob's head. The CIA agent rolled away just in time.

And had to keep on rolling as Chingis followed him, still stomping.

His rolling got stopped by bumping into the prone form of Jana, who was at least alive but fumbling in her purse of all things.

Jacob was about to use his last breath to say something witty and cutting when the archaeologist pulled out the pen gun and fired it at Chingis.

The bullet got him right in the upper chest. The Kyrgyz clutched the wound, then roared.

It was only a .22, after all.

Jacob reached into his pocket for a weapon, but all he came up with was one of the stun grenades. He had forgotten his pistol had gotten lost somewhere in the melee.

Chingis reached for him, a bleeding, leering apparition. Jacob pulled the pin and held the stun grenade in front of the killer's face.

Chingis stared at it a moment, surprised, then his face cracked into a grin and he laughed.

Jacob hadn't let go of the lever that would arm the grenade and set it off in two seconds, but if Chingis thrashed him like he most certainly wanted to, Jacob would let go and it would go off.

And at that range, the stun grenade might very well kill them both.

Why Chingis thought that was funny was something Jacob didn't want to dwell on.

Even so, Jacob found himself laughing along as he struggled to his feet, still holding the grenade. Jana got to her feet too. She didn't seem to find any of this funny at all.

Chingis and Jacob, still laughing, faced off with one another. Jacob waggled the grenade in front of him. Chingis tried to snatch it from him but Jacob was too quick for him.

Slowly, Jacob and Jana backed toward the door. The sounds of fighting died down around them as people noticed what he held in his hand.

"This is an experimental high explosive incendiary grenade!" Jacob announced. "Straight out of a secret American military lab! It's strong enough to blow the foundations off this building."

Chingis laughed even louder. "Lying American. I recognize that model. It's a cheap Yugoslav knockoff of an old Soviet antiriot grenade."

"No, it isn't," Jacob said, still backing away with Jana.

"Yes, it is."

"Let's see who's right." Jacob tossed it across the room at Hassan, who was aiming for him with that shotgun.

Everyone dove for cover, some behind pillars, some underneath tables, as Jacob and Jana bolted for the door.

Jacob tore the door open and pushed Jana out ahead of him.

Right into the arms of the sentry, who had a gun in his hand and murder in his eyes.

A roar behind him told him that Chingis had decided to follow.

Just then there was a loud thud, and a shockwave slammed Chingis into Jacob, both of them into Jana and the sentry, and all four into the opposite wall of the alley.

And Jacob did the worst thing possible in that situation. He blacked out.

CHAPTER TWENTY

Jacob returned to consciousness to find himself in the middle of a pile of bodies. With a grunt he shoved Chingis off him, looked down and found himself tangled with Jana, who was still sleeping it off. The old man who had been keeping watch was down for the count as well. Both looked a bit battered, but not badly hurt.

Jacob staggered to his feet, blinking one eye as some blood trickled into it. His or someone else's? He wasn't sure and didn't have time to check. Through the ringing in his hears he heard police sirens wailing in the distance, coming closer.

He couldn't have been out long. No one had come to investigate the alley, and the police weren't here yet. He had no doubt someone had called them the moment the shooting started. Plus Chingis was still unconscious. Jacob was amazed he'd woken up first.

With one hand he grabbed the sentry's gun off the ground. A compact .38 revolver. Not his first choice of weapon but better than nothing. With his other hand he grabbed Jana by the wrist and unceremoniously dragged her down the alley. No time for chivalry. They needed to get out of here.

He emerged into the street to find it clearing out. The crowds of a few minutes before had dissipated into a few fleeing figures and a city block of closed windows and doors. The people of Lebanon had long since learned to lie low when faced with trouble.

Gunfights and police sirens both counted as trouble.

A taxi rushed down the street, the driver staring around, obviously not knowing what had just happened.

He got a quick lesson when a bloody Westerner dragging a Western woman staggered into the middle of the street and leveled a gun at him.

"Do as you're told and you won't get hurt," Jacob announced as he approached the vehicle. The taxi driver kept his hands where Jacob could see them.

Jacob tossed Jana into the back seat and climbed in.

"Get us out of here," he ordered.

The taxi driver let out a yelp. For a second Jacob was confused as to why, and then saw Chingis rushing out of the alley bellowing a battle cry and swinging a table leg he had found somewhere. Maybe it had gotten blown out the door when the grenade went off.

"Move!" Jacob bellowed.

The driver needed no encouragement. He hit the gas. Chingis swung his table leg and shattered the windshield. The taxi swerved, sideswiped a parked car with a teeth-shattering screech of metal, overcompensated to take out three scooters parked on the other side of the road, then evened out and sped away.

Jacob looked over his shoulder. Chingis was still chasing them, waving the table leg over his head.

"Nice friend you got there," Jana said.

"You're awake!"

"I wish I wasn't," Jana moaned, rubbing a large bruise on the side of her face. "That guy didn't pull any punches."

"We're lucky to be alive."

"Is that a police siren I hear?"

"Yes." Jacob switched back to Arabic. "Driver, get us to the old quarter and drop us off. We'll take it from there."

"The police are coming," the driver said. "And if a traffic officer sees this windshield, he'll stop me. You're not going to shoot at the police, are you?"

"The cops are going to come down the main road to the west of us to respond to the fight we just left behind. Take the back roads. We can avoid them easily enough."

"And what of the traffic police? I don't want to be in the middle of a gunfight."

"You're a lot tougher than the last taxi driver I kidnapped," Jacob said with admiration. "Most people don't talk back to a man holding a gun."

The cabbie shrugged. "I'm from Lebanon."

"The last guy was from Syria."

The cabbie clicked his tongue. "Syrians are weak and stupid."

Jacob smiled, pulled out a stack worth $500, and threw it on the front seat.

"For your trouble, my friend."

The cabbie's eyebrows shot up. "For this, I would drive you to Kabul."

"Don't give him any ideas," Jana said, still nursing her bruises.

"Just drive us to the historic quarter." Jacob gave him an address not far from the hotel. He didn't want to have the guy drop them off too close, but beaten up as they were, he didn't want to walk too far and attract a lot of attention either.

He leaned back in his seat, casting a sympathetic eye on Jana. She was rattled, beaten up, and obviously afraid, but she was holding it together.

Most definitely Aaron Peters's flesh and blood.

"You did good back there," he told her.

"I guess." She looked down. "We didn't find out anything, though."

"Maybe, maybe not."

The only thing they had learned was from that ex-French Foreign Legion soldier, whose trick with the bottle was making Jacob's left arm throb. Absentmindedly he pulled out a compact First Aid kit from his jacket pocket, rolled up his tattered sleeve, and began to dress the wounds, still thinking.

Before the whole situation had gone south, the guy had said something interesting. He had been training The Sword of the Righteous in the Syrian desert. That was one of their strongholds. Made sense. But then they had let him go, saying they were moving operations and acting all hush-hush about it. Somehow he had found out they were moving to the Sinai.

And that's what made Jacob's ears perk up. The Sinai was of huge strategic importance and a hotbed of illegal activity. That's why he had asked what part of the Sinai they had gone to.

Because that would give him a clue as to what they were up to.

The Sinai Peninsula was Egyptian territory. If the terrorists had moved to the northeast part, they might be planning attacks on neighboring Israel, or taking over gunrunning operations into the Gaza Strip. Southern Sinai, and they were probably looking for isolation and to tap into the Bedouin smuggling network.

Northwestern Sinai was the possibility that gave him the most worry. A branch of ISIS had infiltrated that region, and while the Egyptian army had smacked them down hard, elements of that foul death cult remained.

Was The Sword of the Righteous trying to muscle in? And did they have their eyes on the Suez Canal that ran right along Sinai's northwestern edge?

Because if they had a nuke, that would be a global game changer.

Damn it, why did Chingis have to interrupt just when I was going to get some important intel!

Then something the Lebanese mercenary had said jogged his memory. He said he didn't deal with the group because he was a Shiite and The Sword of the Righteous, like ISIS, wanted to kill all Shiites.

The center of the Shiite brand of Islam was Iran.

And there was an American force gathering against Iran right now.

He hadn't been paying much attention to that operation because he had been assigned to other threats, but hadn't he heard that some ships had been peeled off the Atlantic fleet to go to the Persian Gulf?

The quickest way to do that would be to pass through the Suez Canal.

And if they did that, The Sword of the Righteous wouldn't have to get too close to set off their nuke and take those ships out.

And who would the U.S. blame? The Iranians.

Starting a war that would claim thousands of Shiite lives. Maybe even a full-scale invasion that would tie American troops down in a bloodier occupation than they had seen in Afghanistan or even Iraq.

The Shiites would suffer. The West would suffer. Hell, everyone would suffer, because the radiation would block a major shipping route for months. Back in 2021, a container ship had gotten wedged in the Suez Canal for only six days and caused nearly ten billion dollars in lost trade revenue. What would six months do to the global economy?

Global recession. Food shortages. Starvation in the Third World. Persecution of Shiite minorities in Egypt, Lebanon, and all the other Middle Eastern nations, which would force Shiite terror groups to make reprisals, causing more persecution.

Before the dust settled, millions, perhaps tens of millions, would die.

Jacob leaned forward to speak to the cabbie. "I've changed my mind. Take us directly to our hotel. I need to make a phone call. Now."

CHAPTER TWENTY ONE

Professor Meyer died quickly, just as they had promised him.

And just as they had promised him, they would leave his relatives alone. Their European operatives had better things to do than kill some German unbelievers. Those vermin would get what was coming to them in due time.

Ahmed, the Ph.D. physics student who had quit his graduate program at Stanford to wage jihad against those who would oppress true Islam, sat in the back of the truck with the bomb as it sped down an isolated desert road. Professor Meyer had done his job well, and in just under ten hours. There hadn't been much to do, just test the uranium to make sure the ancients had refined it properly, and then fit it into the bomb and make sure the detonator was properly adjusted. It was connected to a timer that could be set to up to twelve hours or as little as one second. Once the timer got down to zero, there'd be a thirty-kiloton explosion.

That was about twice as much as the historic explosion at Hiroshima. Small by modern standards, but good enough for their purposes.

He smiled at Omar and Hamza sitting in the back of the truck with him. Fellow students, fellow jihadists. Not as tough as the warriors who rode up front, but they would kill far more unbelievers. Soon all three of them would enjoy the fruits of paradise together.

In Omar's hands, a Geiger counter softly clicked. They had not had the time to make the bomb entirely sealed from radiation. Even now it was beginning to break apart their DNA and work on their cell walls. They would start feeling symptoms in a day or two.

It didn't matter. In less than that time they would all be drinking honey and laying with *houris*.

Ahmed glanced out the back of the truck, where the sunset had turned the desert a deep red. He checked his watch. Less than an hour until darkness. The Suez Canal wasn't far now. They would approach under cover of darkness, pretending to be an engineering crew working on a canal-side development scheme. The construction project was entirely staffed by members of The Sword of the Righteous. Once safe on site, they would signal the motor boat to pick them up and ferry them and the bomb to the container ship.

While Allah had smiled upon their noble work, he rewarded those who planned well. Faith alone would not win the war. He and his fellow jihadists needed to cover every possible scenario.

They could not be sure the American warships would come through the canal. Perhaps the heretics in Iran would show their cowardice and release the American prisoners. Perhaps the president would send the Army Rangers or Navy SEALs to rescue them. Or perhaps the American spies would figure out enough of his group's plans to warn the fleet away. In any of those cases, the warships would turn around and return to the Atlantic, and they would be left with no target.

So if the target didn't come to them, they would have to go to the target.

The darkness began to gather over the desert. They would wait until morning to transfer the bomb to the waiting ship. America's puppet government in Egypt checked all motor launches at night. During the day they were more lax, there being too many to check.

Ahmed sent up a silent prayer that the Americans would not turn around, that they would arrive in the morning on schedule. The Sword of the Righteous's work would be far, far more effective if they blew up the ships in the canal.

Because then the whole world would ally against the heretics and they would be wiped from the face of the earth.

"It is all your will, oh Victorious One. Let your infinite grace guide our hands to give the heretics and unbelievers a righteous retribution."

* * *

"What do you mean, they need more evidence?" Jacob shouted into the encrypted satellite phone.

"I told you to get more solid intel," his boss Tyler Wallace replied, "and all you got me was an offhand remark by a man who's facing the death penalty in five countries."

"But it all makes sense," Jacob shot back. He glanced at Jana, who stood guard at the door of his hotel room. He felt no need for secrecy at this point. She was all in, and might as well listen to the conversation.

Not that he'd mention that to the CIA. This was a serious breach of protocol that could land them both in jail.

None of that mattered at the moment. Time was everything, and he needed every bit of help he could get.

"Look, Jacob, you convinced me already. While the idea of uranium 235 hidden in an ancient artifact sounds crazy, it's the only explanation for why The Sword of the Righteous would go to such lengths. And satellite data does show that a training base for an unidentified militant group did get abandoned a few months ago in the eastern Syrian desert near Palmyra. But we don't have intel on which group that was, and we haven't found evidence of any new activity in the Sinai."

"Of course not. There's so much going on over there nobody can keep track of it all. These guys are good at hiding, great at covering their tracks."

"All the more reason you need something more concrete if you want to get the higher-ups on board. All you have right now is a hunch, Jacob. A hunch I happen to share. But they're not going to launch a major operation on the basis of a hunch from one field agent. Especially when that agent has such a strange story. The regional director actually laughed at me."

Jacob groaned. Wallace was right, of course. You couldn't take operatives needed for vital operations elsewhere and have them fly off to the Suez to look for a bomb that could be absolutely anywhere, or might not exist at all. And he would have laughed at the story too if he hadn't been on the ground investigating it himself.

"When does the flotilla arrive at the mouth of the Suez Canal?"

"0930 tomorrow morning."

Jacob checked his watch. They had enough time to get to the canal and have a few hours to search.

A few hours, when they needed several days.

"Can you fly us to Port Said?" Jacob asked.

"Orhan Yildirim is still in Beirut. I'll give him a call. That's the most I can do."

"Can you get me a helicopter once we're there? It would help our search."

"What did I just say?"

"Wallace, come *on*."

Deep sigh. "I'll see what I can do."

"Have him get us a Geiger counter," Jana said.

"Is someone in the room with you?" Wallace asked.

Jacob waved her to be silent and got a frown in return. "No. Just some tourists in the street outside. Can you get us a Geiger counter?"

"Good thinking, Jacob. They might not have the ability to make the bomb totally sealed. I'll make sure the field office gives you a top of the line model."

"Thank you." He gave Jana a thumb's up.

"But if their nuke really is leaking, it wouldn't be leaking much, otherwise it would kill them before they could transport it. You'd have to get the Geiger counter up close to detect it."

"I know, but it's better than nothing." A terrible thought occurred to him. "Wallace, are any of the ships carrying nukes?"

Jana whirled around, jaw dropping.

Long pause.

"I'm not at liberty to say," his boss mumbled.

That's a yes.

"Jesus, if a nuke goes off close enough, it might set off the rest!"

"I'm not an expert, but it would have to be pretty close," Wallace said.

"Within a mile? Within a couple of hundred yards?"

"I don't know."

And it didn't matter all that much. Because even if the American nukes didn't go off, the explosion would break them apart, spreading uranium 235 all over the canal zone, irradiating it for years and requiring a multibillion dollar clean-up plan, during which no sea traffic could get through.

"Damn," Jacob said. "Even if they only succeed halfway they'll have succeeded more than they ever expected."

"I'll get you on that plane," Wallace said. "Head straight for the airport. I'll make sure Orhan's waiting for you. We'll get you to Egypt as quick as we can."

"That probably won't be quick enough," Jacob said, hanging up.

CHAPTER TWENTY TWO

As soon as Orhan touched down in Port Said on the northern end of the Suez Canal in Egypt, Jacob got back on the satellite phone to his boss.

"You get me that chopper?" he asked.

"Yes. Just a small private model. It's all I could swing. Probably better because it will be inconspicuous. It's waiting for you at the airport."

"Great. What's the status of the fleet?"

"It's arriving at Port Said in two hours."

"Jesus, Wallace. You've got to get them turned around. There's no way we're going to find the bomb in that time. The canal is 120 miles long and it could be on either side!"

He had examined satellite images of the canal on their sleepless flight. The canal passed through three cities, long stretches of farmland, and a large lake dotted with islands. Despite a heavy Egyptian army presence, it would be child's play to plant a bomb somewhere along its length. Given the blast radius, even a small bomb planted a mile away would destroy the fleet.

"You know I don't have the authority to stop the fleet," Wallace said, "and no one who does believes you."

Orhan parked his plane near the hanger. The helipads were arrayed on a dusty stretch a little beyond. Jacob and Jana hopped out, moving toward the helicopters. Jacob held the satellite phone while Jana struggled with their bags and a heavy bag of armaments Orhan had given them.

"Can you patch me through to the flotilla commander?" Jacob asked.

"Sure. It will take the techies a minute."

"I'll wait."

They continued walking toward the helipads.

"I just thought of something," Jana said, huffing along with her heavy load, sweat pouring down her face despite the early hour.

"What?"

"The terrorists wouldn't want to risk missing the fleet."

"The canal is so narrow they can't. Not with a nuke."

107

"That's not what I mean. You're trying to get the fleet turned around. Well, they'd worry about that. The terrorists know they're being watched. They know the theft and murders are being investigated. They'd worry that you might figure things out and turn the warships around before they entered the canal. They wouldn't want to risk that. So they'd put the bomb on a boat."

Jacob stopped short. "My God, you're right."

What an idiot I am! I should have figured that out. Chingis must have given me a concussion or something.

"But how can we find out which boat it's on?" Jana asked.

"Damn good question," Jacob said, rubbing his chin, which badly needed a shave. "But that's a good insight of yours. That helps. Thank you."

"You can thank me by carrying one of these bags."

Just then Wallace got back on the line. "We're patching you through to the *USS Brandywine* now."

"Thanks," Jacob said, striding for the helipad once again. Jana rolled her eyes and struggled to keep up.

A new voice came over the line. "Captain Arnold Cranston of the *USS Brandywine* speaking."

"Hello captain, this is Agent Jacob Snow of the Central Intelligence Agency. I have some vital intel for you."

Jacob proceeded to tell the captain everything he knew. He explained in detail, standing well away from the helipads, alone in the desert, as Jana dealt with the airport bureaucracy and got clearance for the helicopter to take off.

Once Jacob's explanation was finished, Captain Cranston fell silent for a moment.

"Agent Snow, to be honest I'm not sure if I believe your story. But you're the man on the ground and you believe it. You wouldn't be asking for such a move if you weren't one hundred percent. Unfortunately, I cannot turn the flotilla around without direct orders from the secretary of defense or the president himself."

"But, sir—"

"I am sorry, Agent Snow, but there's nothing I can do. I'll send the request upstairs, but I don't give it much chance of being taken seriously. Rest assured that we will keep up our guard. I'll double the watch on all decks, and we've liaised with our Egyptian allies to make sure they're taking due vigilance. Your superior informed me that you will be scouting with a helicopter. The Egyptians are aware of this and will not fire upon you."

"That's reassuring. Are they providing air support?"

"I'm afraid not. But they have taken the unusual precaution of halting all traffic through the canal until we're through."

"All traffic has been cleared?"

"That's right. All ships are either moored outside Port Said at the north end or Port Suez at the south end. I believe some are moored at Great Bitter Lake in the middle."

"Then that's where they'll hit! You'll have to pass right by them and there's no Egyptian naval base there."

"We can't know they even have the capability you think they do, agent." Captain Cranston sounded like he was struggling to maintain his patience.

"Thank you, sir, and good luck."

Jacob hung up. He didn't want to waste any more precious time trying to convince someone who didn't even have the authority to turn his own ship around.

Jacob sprinted to the awaiting helicopter, a small, fast two-seater. An Egyptian ground crew was just leaving. Jana had already stowed the bags.

"They told me everything's prepared and it's fully fueled," she said. "And we're cleared for takeoff."

"Thanks." Jacob got behind the controls and switched on the motor. Above them, the rotors began to turn. Soon they lifted off and soared high above the port, a mass of concrete buildings stretching out before them, the blue of the Mediterranean to the north, and a 200-meter-wide channel of water leading from it out of sight to the south.

Jacob caught a glimpse of a line of sleek gray vessels approaching Port Said. His heart sunk. The American flotilla.

He swung the helicopter around and skimmed low over the canal, heading south.

"The captain told me they've cleared the traffic," he told Jana. "Some ships are at Great Bitter Lake about 50 miles south of here. I'm going to check those out."

Jana rummaged through the bag Orhan had given them and came out with an M16. Setting that aside, she pulled out a hunting rifle with a high-powered scope. She checked the magazine and flicked off the safety.

"Know your way around one of those?" Jacob asked, glancing at her. The way she handled it, she certainly seemed to.

"You wouldn't believe the arsenal we had in our basement."

"Actually I would."

109

"Well, you knew him better than I did," Jana growled.

Jacob took a deep breath. The canal was clear as far as he could see. No ship traffic at all. He kept the helicopter at top speed.

"Look, Jana. Since there's a good chance you, me, and everyone in a five-mile radius might die in the next hour, I think it might be good for you to forgive him."

"Forgive him! Why should I forgive a single parent who abandons his child?"

"He told me it was you who cut him off."

"I gave him an ultimatum. I was tired off all the broken promises, all the missed graduations and birthdays. I told him if he wasn't home for my twenty-first birthday, he might as well not come home at all."

"I know. He told me. It was the biggest regret of his life, but he had a duty to perform."

Jana sneered. "Duty! You sound just like him. Any time he wanted to duck some personal responsibility, he always came up with a duty to perform."

"He had something important to do that day."

"And what the hell was more important than his daughter?"

Saving me.

"That's classified," he mumbled.

"You guys are all the same. Hiding behind your machismo and some oh-so-important special ops. Sometimes I think the tough guys are the biggest cowards of all."

Jacob flushed, thinking of all the relationships he'd dodged, the friendships he'd let go stale. Fighting bad guys came easier than dealing with good people.

But what she said wasn't fair. Not one person in a thousand could do what he did, and it kept the other 999 safe.

They flew on in silence, on and on down the barren stretch of water, farmer's fields and the occasional town on each side. Jacob had flown along the canal many times before, and it had always been full of freighters, cruise liners, oil tankers, and container ships. It was eerie to see it empty.

He flew low, not wanting to miss any detail. A small powerboat could carry a nuke just as easily as one of the bigger ships. Hell, now that the ships had all been stopped they might have gotten spooked and packed the nuke in that mosque over there, or in that collection of a dozen farmers' huts just down the road from it. Or somewhere in that town of a few thousand people coming up ahead.

110

It could be anywhere, simply anywhere, and that Geiger counter would be useless unless they were standing within a few yards of it.

Jacob felt a rising sense of panic. He tamped it down and focused on the job.

If only he knew how to perform it.

His satellite phone rang. With one hand on the controls, he picked it up.

"Agent Snow."

Wallace's voice came over the line. "Any luck?"

"No, sir."

"I was calling to inform you that the flotilla, led by the *USS Brandywine*, has entered the canal."

Jacob took a deep breath and let it out slowly. "Thank you, sir."

Wallace didn't need to say any more. The canal was too narrow for large ships to turn around, and a group of ships that big would take more than a mile just to stop. There was no turning back now.

If that bomb was anywhere up ahead, he and Jana needed to find it, otherwise thousands would die today, and millions would die this year.

CHAPTER TWENTY THREE

Jacob circled around the Great Bitter Lake, an expansive body of salt water almost directly at the midpoint of the Suez Canal. To both sides, large ships sat moored in long lines, creating a two half-circles of metal gleaming in the sunlight close to the shore.

He stared at each one in turn, and couldn't see anything unusual on any of them.

But of course there wouldn't be. A band of terrorists smart and dedicated enough to make their own nuke could cover up their occupation of a ship easily enough. There had been no mayday calls. When they took over the ship, they had done it quickly enough that no one had sounded the alarm.

Took over? Maybe they even owned the thing. It could be an entire ship filled with terrorists.

Wonderful.

At least none of the ships were moving. That gave Jacob some time. If the terrorists were laying low, waiting for the fleet to come to them, he might just have enough time to find out which one the bomb was on.

The only problem with that was that there was no way of telling. The Geiger counter sat between the seats, switched on but silent. No way would it pick up anything at this distance.

Jana broke into his thoughts. "Have you noticed there's no traffic on the roads?"

Jacob looked around. He had been so focused on the canal he hadn't noticed. Stupid mistake. This mission had gotten him rattled.

"You're right. The Egyptians must have halted it."

"I saw a roadblock a couple of miles back on the right bank. Didn't think anything of it until now. There are no vehicles at all."

Jacob scanned the area, his gaze running up and down the canal-side highways running along either bank. His heart skipped as he saw in the distance on the left bank a lone truck with a canvas canopy on the back, headed north.

Headed toward the fleet.

He swept the helicopter down and over, chasing the truck. His mind raced. If the terrorists saw the chopper, they might detonate the bomb early.

That was fine, because their current position was far enough south that it wouldn't take out the fleet.

It would only destroy the canal, disrupting global trade and starting a Sunni-Shiite war that would kill millions.

Jacob gritted his teeth. There was no getting around it. They had to stop the bombers before they set it off.

But how to do that?

"Jana, have you ever fired at anyone?"

"What?" She sounded nervous.

"You know your way around a gun, but have you ever shot to kill?"

"No." Now she sounded really nervous.

"You're going to have to in about thirty seconds when we catch up to these guys. They're going fast. Aim for the tires. Maybe you can make them career off the road and crash. Then shoot every one of them you can. I'll land as soon as possible and fire on them too. Can you do that?"

"Y-yes."

"Jana. If you don't kill these guys right now, millions will die. Including us."

"I know," she said, her voice coming out so quiet that if it weren't for the radio earphones he would have never heard her.

"Can you do it?"

They were almost in range. No reaction from the truck. Either the terrorists hadn't seen them or thought they wouldn't get fired on. Jacob wasn't flying a police or military chopper, after all, just a civilian model.

Jacob veered a bit over the water so Jana could get a clear shot at the wheels.

He could only see the driver, an old man in a keffiyeh and a white beard who kept glancing at the helicopter.

No way this guy is a civilian. There are roadblocks everywhere. The Egyptians sealed every street. He and his buddies hidden in back must have shot their way through the last roadblock. They'll shoot through the next one too, and on and on until they get to the fleet.

And if the soldiers stop them, they'll simply detonate the bomb early.

"Can you do it?" Jacob repeated.

Jana aimed the rifle. The driver looked again, mouth opening, shouting something they couldn't hear.

Jana didn't fire.

"Jana! Now!"

113

The rifle barked. The truck swerved, then got back in its lane.

She had missed.

Jana racked the bolt and aimed again. Jacob kept quiet. Why weren't they returning fire?

Jana fired a second round. The front tire shredded. The truck swerved, the old man tried to compensate, and ended up hitting the drainage ditch on the other side of the road.

His truck toppled over. The canvas tarp on the back flew off, and hundreds of cantaloupes tumbled out.

No terrorists, no bomb, just hundreds and hundreds of cantaloupes.

Jacob brought the helicopter around and hovered over the wreck. Cantaloupes rolled in both directions along the drainage ditch, making it look like a flood of melons. The entire back had emptied out, and he could see no people or suspicious objects in the back. Just cantaloupes.

The old man crawled out of the truck's cab, shaking his fist at the helicopter and shouting something.

"Whoops," Jacob said. "Sorry about that."

"Oh my God. At least he's OK," Jana said.

"That's what he gets for ignoring police advice." Jacob gained altitude.

"Don't be mean. He's probably some policeman's father who allowed him to pass."

"Yeah, probably." In this part of the world, family connections could bend a lot of rules. Whatever idiot bent the rules in this case was going to get a serious chewing out from his superior officer, not to mention his dad.

Jacob looked around, unsure what to do next. Jana looked too.

"Is that a wake?" she asked.

"Where?"

Before she could answer he spotted it too. At the edge of their vision to the south, they could see a large container ship moored along the edge of Great Bitter Lake had moved out of the line and was cutting towards the center of the lake, its wake a white V behind it.

"That must be them!" Jacob shouted.

"That's a big boat. It will take them ages to get up to speed."

"Doesn't matter. The fleet can't turn around. Even if they stop, they're trapped."

Jacob brought the chopper up to a higher altitude to seem less threatening and moved in the ship's direction, angling over the land in the hopes that the terrorists would think they weren't a threat.

That won't last when I try to approach, Jacob realized.

Jana fed two more rounds into the rifle to top it up. Despite shooting at the wrong guy, she seemed calmer now, more focused. She had, Jacob knew from bitter experience, crossed a line. She had assumed that poor bastard back there was a terrorist, and shot at him. Hesitation and fear had been overcome, and now that she faced what they felt sure was the real set of terrorists, she wouldn't hesitate this time.

But she wasn't fully trained, no matter how much Aaron had shown her. Jana didn't have the intense conditioning and field experience a Ranger or CIA operative did. She was useful, but could not replace a real fighter.

She's all you got. You have to fly the chopper.

As they sped down the canal, the cargo ship looming closer and closer, Jacob fearing that it would go off in a blinding flare at any moment, a flashing blue and red light by the shore caught his eye.

A police patrol boat came speeding out from a small dock in pursuit. It ate up the distance between it and the slower-moving container ship, no doubt blaring a loudspeaker order to stop that Jacob couldn't hear over the sound of the rotors.

Several figures, tiny as ants, scurried along the sides of the container ship, heading for the rear of the boat. Just as the police patrol pulled up behind and moved to the right to get beside the container ship, several sparks lit up from larger vessel.

Small arms fire.

The police returned fire. Jacob squinted to see the details. He was still too far to make out much.

Jacob wasn't too far to miss the bright flare, plume of smoke, and quick blur as the terrorists fired an RPG at the patrol boat.

The explosion hit directly on the cabin. The patrol boat swerved, cutting a tight circle, but this was no evasive maneuver. Whoever had been at the helm must have been killed instantly.

Still, the terrorists took no chances. As a couple of tiny figures leapt from the police vessel into the water, the RPG fired a second time, hitting the boat below the waterline. It listed to port and began to sink.

"What do we do?" Jana asked.

"We're going to attack," Jacob replied. "We're going to fly right over the container ship and you're going to fire on those guys until they take cover. Then we're going to land and try to find the bomb."

He looked at Jana to gauge her reaction. She looked back at him like he'd just come up with the craziest idea in the world. And he had.

The problem was, he couldn't think of a better plan.

115

"What if they set off the nuke now?" Jana asked. Her voice sounded worried, but did not crack.

Impressive. You really are a lot like your old man.

"We won't be able to get away in time, even if I fly away now. So let's go for it."

Pause. "All right."

"They must have had a spotter up in Port Said to tell them the flotilla had entered the canal. That's why they started out. They want to be close enough to catch them in the kill zone, and didn't want to risk waiting for the flotilla coming here. They must have figured we're on to them. But they won't hit the button if they think they can fight us off."

Jana gave a quick, nervous nod. Jacob did not follow up with what else he thought.

That if he and his half-trained assistant, by some miracle, managed to land on the ship and overwhelm at least part of its crew, whoever was watching the bomb would set it off rather than risk the chance of the bomb being captured.

So if they fled, disaster. If they tried to take the ship and failed, disaster. If they landed on the ship and began to win, disaster.

But at least they could keep it from setting off the American nukes.

And maybe, just maybe, they could overwhelm the terrorists before they set off the bomb.

Jacob didn't share with his partner just how unlikely he thought that outcome was.

Jana readied her hunting rifle. Jacob swooped over the container ship for an initial pass as the terrorists on board saw them and got into position.

I should have gone on that sailing trip with Gabriella.

CHAPTER TWENTY FOUR

Jacob gritted his teeth as the terrorists opened fire. The container ship was as tall and as long as a city block of apartment buildings. He had no idea how he and Jana were going to find the nuke among all those thousands of containers, but that was a problem for after he managed to land.

In the meantime, he swung the chopper from side to side, trying to dodge the fire coming from half a dozen locations on the boat.

They flew over the prow first. A figure ran along the narrow walkway between the starboard gunwale and the side of the container stack, raising what looked like an AK-47.

Jana aimed and fired. This time, she didn't hesitate.

She didn't hit, either.

The man flinched, then fired a burst back. None of the bullets hit the chopper.

Jacob risked flying in straight to give Jana a better firing platform, and when her rifle barked a second time, the figure jerked back and fell on the deck.

"Nice one!"

Jacob winced. That had come out automatically. For a fellow soldier, it counted as encouragement; for a civilian it might sound ghoulish or make her self-conscious.

No need to worry about that. Jana racked the bolt and aimed again. Two more figures appeared, one on each side of the boat. These were more careful, getting to one knee to make a smaller target and, judging from the flares coming from the muzzles of their AK-47s, firing single shots rather than three-round bursts. Jacob had used AKs on a number of occasions and the weapon, while durable, was too light for its caliber. Firing a burst sacrificed accuracy, so much so that firing on full automatic was nicknamed "spray and pray."

A loud pang, audible over the rotors, told him one of the guys had made a hit.

Jana fired, missed, racked the bolt, and fired again.

One of the figures jerked, dropping his gun and grasping his forearm.

"Good job. Keep firing!" Jacob shouted.

His civilian assistant needed no encouragement. She fired again without hesitation. Getting shot at was a good motivator even for the greenest of civilians, and Aaron had made sure his daughter was as experienced as he could make her.

The helicopter passed over the prow of the ship, flying only about 300 feet above the top of the container stack, Jacob searching for evidence of the bomb.

All he saw was row upon row of shipping containers.

What if it's in one of the bottom ones where we can't get at it? They might have put it on a timer and sealed it under a mass of steel.

A more immediate problem came from a guy running along the top of the containers right in front of them, hopping the narrow space to the next one as he got to the end of each, spraying his AK on full auto.

Another couple of impacts on the helicopter, one on the body and another spiderwebbing the windshield.

Damn it, he must be praying extra hard.

Not enough. Jana took him out with a headshot.

Was that luck? That must have been luck.

They swept past the body as it tumbled into the narrow space between two shipping containers and vanished. Out of the corner of his eye Jacob saw someone else firing, but they were already leaving him behind as they sped for the ship's stern.

They passed it and ended up over open water. Jacob glanced at the controls, didn't see any warning lights from the shots they'd taken, and banked around for another pass.

Two figures stood at the rear of the boat to greet them. One had a rifle, not an AK but what looked like a rifle with a scope.

To his left stood the guy with the rocket-propelled grenade.

Jacob made a quick decision.

"Get the guy on the left!"

"But the guy on the right has—"

"The left!"

Just then, both men fired simultaneously. The windshield cracked again as the sniper put a bullet right between them. Through the countless cracks on the plexiglass he saw the telltale flash and plume of smoke as the RPG went off.

Jacob banked hard to the left. The projectile blurred past. Jana flinched.

"Jesus!"

"Keep firing!" Jacob ordered. "The only way to stay safe is to keep firing!"

By the time Jana got it together, they had already passed the stern of the ship and were flying over the center. A terrorist knelt atop one of the containers, taking steady shots at the helicopter. None hit. Firing at a moving object in the air was difficult and took training, but it was only a matter of time before these guys hit the engine or the rotors.

Or one of them.

Jana fired three shots as they flew past. None of them hit.

Damn. She's rattled. No fault of hers but we don't have time for this.

He made a hard turn, corkscrewing up to gain altitude.

"Jana. We need to land. They might set off the bomb at any moment. But before we land we have to take out the guy with the RPG. He could take us out with a single shot as we land. So we're going back there. I'm going to keep the chopper as still as I can, and you're going to shoot him. All right?"

"All right."

"Reload."

"What? Oh!" Jana shook herself, realizing she had forgotten that crucial step. As she fed the rounds in, Jacob noticed a flashing red light on the dashboard.

Critically low fuel.

One of those shots must have cut the fuel line. It's a miracle we didn't blow up.

"We've got one chance at this, Jana."

He brought the chopper around to just behind the back of the container ship, which he could see was picking up speed, and began to descend.

The man with the RPG was climbing a ladder to get to the top of the shipping container stack, his weapon strapped to his back. Jacob did not see the man with the sniper's rifle.

Jacob descended as low as he dared and turned the helicopter so Jana would have a comfortable shot.

She fired. A spark flashed on the metal side of the shipping container next to the terrorist. He flinched and then kept on climbing.

Jan racked the bolt and aimed …

… and then Jacob spotted the sniper.

He stood on deck, tucked between two shipping containers and only showing his head and shoulders, his gun aimed right at them.

The terrorist fired. Sparks flew from the dashboard. Jacob struggled to control the chopper as it jiggled crazily in the air. Jana tried to fire but the chopper had become too unstable. The terrorist with the RPG got to the top of the container stack, turned, and unslung his RPG, a grin on his face.

The chopper began to descend of its own volition. Cursing, Jacob wrestled with the controls. He yanked hard on them, trying to keep the dying bird from slamming into the back of the container stack.

Directly in front of him, the terrorist aimed, his mouth moving, probably in prayer.

Jacob cleared the container stack by inches, slamming into the terrorist.

The ravaged plexiglass gave way, and the terrorist's battered body landed in Jana's lap.

Just then the helicopter's landing skids hit the top of the container. The helicopter juddered, turning and threatening to tip over. If the still-spinning rotors hit the surface, they'd smash and probably decapitate them both.

Jacob hauled on the controls, trying to gain a final second of maneuverability.

The chopper leveled out, raised a few inches, and fell straight down onto the container with a loud clang. The rotors whined as the power cut off. The cabin filled with the smell of gasoline as the tank's last reserves leaked in an expanding pool onto the shipping container.

Jana shoved the body of the terrorist off her. It slumped half out of the hole it had made in the windshield, its shattered limbs like twisted branches.

Jacob tore into the duffel bag of weapons provided by the local CIA office and found the usual things. He grabbed an MP5 submachinegun and a spare clip for it, a 9mm pistol with holster, and hesitated when he saw the stun and fragmentation grenades. Could he dare use them close to a nuclear bomb? He grabbed a few of each anyway, stuffing his vest pockets with them.

Jacob handed Jana another 9mm pistol and holster.

"Take that M16," he told her. "The hunting rifle is no good for close up work."

She did as he told her. Jacob fished into the bag a little more and brought out two walkie talkies.

"Take one of these. They're encrypted. The terrorists won't be able to listen in. Just don't change the channel."

"How the hell are we going to find the bomb in time?" she asked as she jumped out of the chopper and into the pool of gasoline. The rotors, still spinning although slowing down, spattered it all over them. She had the Geiger counter slung over one shoulder.

"No idea. Hopefully you're right and that bomb's a bit leaky. Work your way along the ship. I'm going to run to the prow and commandeer the bridge. I need to stop this ship."

Jana's eyes went wide. "We're going to split up?"

Jacob ran around the chopper, put a hand on her shoulder, and looked her in the eye. "You can do it. I know you and your father had your differences, but he loved you, and he'd be damn proud to see the way you've acted today."

Instead of being reassured by this, her eyes widened further.

"Look out!" she shouted, raising her M16.

Jacob spun around, and saw a terrorist standing about fifty yards away, his Kalashnikov leveled.

But he wasn't aiming for them.

He was aiming for the pool of gasoline at their feet.

CHAPTER TWENTY FIVE

Jana and Jacob fired at the same time. The terrorist pirouetted, blood spurting from his chest, and fell.

Jana had no idea if she had killed him or Jacob had. It didn't matter. He was dead.

"Get on it!" Jacob shouted, running for the prow of the ship, hundreds of yards away.

Stinking of gasoline, clutching her M16, the Geiger counter slapping her hip, she ran for the back of the ship. She needed to make a full sweep. Be methodical. How the hell she was going to manage that with a crew of terrorists on board? She had no idea.

The odd thought came to her that she felt an urge to impress this annoying, overly testosterone-ed man. She had stopped trying to impress men after she had given up trying to impress her father, and yet now she was throwing herself into danger and one of the motivations was to get Jacob's approval.

That thought got rudely shoved aside as a terrorist climbing the ladder at the rear stack of shipping containers popped his head over the top just a few paces ahead of her.

Jana fired from the hip, and surprised herself by hitting.

The top of his head exploded, blood, brains, and bits of skull flying back before he plummeted out of sight.

Jana paused, the gorge rising up in her throat. She had shot a few men already, but at a distance. She hadn't seen the blood, except for that terrorist who had crashed through the windshield, and Jacob had killed that one. She had been able to keep a distance from her own actions.

Not anymore.

Her whole body shuddered. Jana gritted her teeth and forced her muscles to obey her command to be still. She didn't have time for this.

Get it together, or you die.

And millions of other people.

What was it that Dad said?

"Always act strong, especially when you feel weak."

She ran up to the rear end of the last container and peeked over. No terrorists in sight, except for the sprawled, bloody body at the foot of the ladder far below.

Jana avoided looking at it.

After a moment, she focused on it, counting slowly to three.

That could be you. Instead, it's him.

The gruesome sight slowly became tolerable.

Shots rang out toward the prow of the ship, a harsh reminder that Jacob was relying on her.

She remembered to crouch, making herself less of a target, and scanned the area. She didn't see anyone alive on her end of the ship. There were two ladders at the stern, one at either side of the ship. The containers were stacked six wide and ten high. Hopefully the ladders would get her close enough to detect any radiation.

But would the Geiger counter detect it at all? Would the metal of the shipping containers stop any radiation from leaking out? Was her hunch that the bomb emitted radiation even correct?

Jana had no idea. All she knew was that she had no choice but to search.

She checked the Geiger counter. The needle didn't move. Slinging the M16 over her shoulder, she swung down onto the ladder and began to descend.

More shots from the direction of the prow. She didn't even look. That man was a killing machine, and hopefully he could hold his own against the crew. She had her own job to do and that would take all her concentration.

She clambered down the ladder, hampered by the unfamiliar feel and weight of the M16 strapped to her back, the pistol in its holster on her belt, and the Geiger counter dangling from her shoulder. The firing from the front of the ship increased, so much so that she worried she wouldn't hear the Geiger counter if it started clicking. She tried to keep an eye on it, as well as the deck below, and the top of the container stack above.

A terrorist could appear any moment, and if he caught her on the ladder, she'd be dead.

At last she made it down to the deck, a good five stories below. She drew her pistol and held the Geiger counter with her other hand. Carefully she peeked around the container stack and down the portside walkway. A moving figure made her duck back, then she looked again. He was running away from her, and had almost made it to the prow of the ship. She saw no one else.

Jana turned and walked along the back of the ship, eyes and ears alert. The needle on the Geiger counter didn't budge.

She got all the way to the other side of the ship and peeked around the container stack to look down the starboard walkway.

A bullet panged off the shipping container side just inches from her head, making her duck back.

She'd only gotten a moment's glimpse of him. All she knew was that he had an AK-47 and was barely fifty yards away. He'd close that distance in a few seconds.

Jana reached around the corner and fired blind with her pistol, emptying the eleven-round magazine in a flurry of shots.

When all she got was the *click* of an empty pistol, she ejected the magazine and reached for her backup.

Only to realize she didn't have a backup.

She fumbled to get her M16 in the ready position, heart hammering in her chest, expecting the terrorist to jump around the corner any moment, gun blazing.

But he didn't.

Once ready, she paused for a moment, gathering her courage, then peeked around the corner, leading with her gun.

The man lay not ten yards from her, riddled with bullets.

She quickly looked away from the bloody mess almost at her feet, like she had avoided looking for too long at the dead man who had fallen from the top of the container stack.

Jana saw no one along the rest of the walkway.

And she didn't hear any more gunfire. That made her worried. Had Jacob been killed?

She felt tempted to radio him, but if he was hiding, that would alert the terrorists to his position.

So not knowing if she was alone on the boat now, she had to make a decision—where next to look for the bomb?

The terrorists would want to place it somewhere they could easily access it. So it was likely not in the middle of the stacks of containers, unless they'd cut secret passages to get to it. Assuming they hadn't done that, then it must be in a container on the back, sides, or front. Or maybe the top, if one of the containers had a hatch. While she hadn't noticed any up there, she hadn't had a chance to look over more than a small fraction of the surface area.

Jana had noticed ladders going up both sides of the stacks from the port and starboard walkways at regular intervals. Normally container ships didn't have that. Since the containers were loaded and unloaded with cranes, there was no need. Obviously The Sword of the Righteous had controlled this ship for some time and wanted to give its crew maximum mobility. They knew they might have to defend it, and get to the bomb, wherever it was, quickly from any point on the ship.

Did that mean it was in one of the top containers? Ladders all along the sides would hint at that. Or maybe it was on one of the sides, and it would be quicker for someone on the opposite side to climb up, run across the top, and climb down.

I could second guess these nutcases all day.

Jana decided to climb back up the starboard rear ladder. She did not think the Geiger counter was strong enough to detect along the entire back of the ship, so she had to make sure it wasn't one of the rear containers. Despite the crazy situation, she needed to go about the search in a rational, methodical fashion, as if she was on an archaeological excavation.

After a final peek around the corner, she tossed her empty pistol aside and climbed the ladder.

The sun was rising higher, the water doubling its heat with a harsh reflection. Sweat poured down her face, but her muscles did not falter. She'd worked for years in the hot sun and her body was up to the challenge.

To her surprise, it seemed her mind was too. She had taken on a clinical distance to the violence. She was scared—no point in denying that—but for some reason the fear didn't stop her.

It reminded her of Brian, the older graduate student on her dig in Morocco she had her eye on, and what he had said to her once.

"I'm scared of heights," he had admitted as they stood atop a cliff overlooking the Strait of Gibraltar.

"We can go somewhere else," she had offered.

He laughed and waved away the suggestion. "It's all right. When I was an undergraduate, all those years ago, I joined the rock climbing club, thinking I could cure my fear of heights. I went climbing every weekend for three years."

"It sure worked."

"No it didn't. I was terrified on every one of those weekends, and spent the whole week dreading it, just like I am now. But I learned to deal with the fear. I can do what I need to do without it affecting my actions or slowing me down. One summer I even took a job as a roofer."

So was that how Jacob dealt with it? Was that how Dad dealt with it? She remembered Dad saying how anyone who claimed not to be scared in battle was either a psychopath or a liar.

Jana Peters got to the top of the container stack without the Geiger counter responding. She peeked over the lip of the top container, at the vast field of identical containers reaching all the way to the prow. She saw nothing except a few dead bodies, those left in Jacob Snow's wake.

She had to run across that wide open area, search it inch by inch while exposed to enemy fire. That sniper who had cut their fuel line was still around somewhere.

No choice. She had to check. If Jacob could do it, if Dad could do it, then so could she.

Jana leapt onto the container and, gripping her M16, moved toward the front of the boat, ears alert for the click of the Geiger counter or the sound of movement from some dedicated maniac intent on killing her and millions of other people.

CHAPTER TWENTY SIX

Jacob's luck had just run out. He'd fought all the way to the front of the ship, killing anyone who came across his path, and then got stopped short.

Ladders ran down both sides of the container stacks at regular intervals, and two ran down the front of the stack, just behind the conning tower that contained the bridge and crew quarters at the very front of the boat, but to try and go down those ladders would have been suicide, because a whole crowd of those nutcases were holed up in there, firing out the portholes.

Jacob lay prone on the top container, firing down at the slightly lower conning tower, but he could make no headway. The portholes were small and those damn walls were bulletproof.

Sooner or later, they'd send guys around both sides to flank him. He couldn't stay in his current position, and he couldn't move forward.

So he had to try a flanking maneuver of his own.

Jacob ran back a hundred yards to one of the ladders on the port side. Peeking over, he saw a pair of terrorists creeping along, hugging the sides of the container, thinking he wouldn't see them.

Sneaky bastards.

He dropped a frag grenade on them, hoping the nuke didn't happened to be nearby.

Nothing blew except the grenade, leaving the terrorists pasted all over the deck and the sides of the containers.

Maybe my luck hasn't run out after all.

We'll see as I climb down this ladder and make myself a perfect target.

He went down as fast as he could, skipping rungs, risking a neck-breaking fall in order to shave off a few seconds of helplessness.

His luck held. Almost.

Out of the corner of his eye, he saw someone running around the port side, aiming a rifle at him.

Oh crap. That sniper.

The sniper fired. Jacob let go of the ladder.

The bullet missed him, but as Jacob's stomach lurched up into his throat, he knew he wouldn't miss the deck.

He picked up speed, plunging toward the steel surface.

Jacob hit the deck and rolled as he had been trained to do, but no amount of training could prepare him for that long fall, or the fact that he landed on the pistol in the holster on his belt and then rolled right over the MP5 strapped to his back.

He rolled to a stop, body aching, pretty sure he had broken something.

No time for that now. That sniper was bound to take another shot.

Jacob had ended up on his front, just inches from a bollard. He scampered behind it, his limbs barely obeying.

A bullet pinged off the bollard the second he got behind it.

He fumbled to get his MP5 into position. At least his arms worked. He wasn't sure about his legs, though.

The sniper lay prone too, half hidden by the corner of the shipping container stack, aiming right at him.

Jacob ducked back as another bullet sought him out, ricocheting off the deck inches away.

Now it was his turn. Ignoring the pain in his hip, he peeked out from behind the bollard and fired his submachine gun.

Or at least he tried to. The damn thing was jammed.

That's what you get for smacking it on the deck from a fall of twenty feet, idiot.

Or was it thirty?

Back he went behind the bollard, an instant before another bullet almost passed through his skull.

Jacob set the MP5 aside and pulled out his pistol. Hopefully it wouldn't jam too. Just as he was about to move out of cover enough to fire, he heard a shot and felt a hot pain on his thigh.

He scrunched behind the bollard even more and inspected his leg. Just a graze, but it told him that the bollard he hid behind wasn't quite big enough to completely obscure him from view.

Time to end this. He reached around and fired a blind shot that would hopefully put the sniper's head down, then revealed his own head so he could see what he was doing.

The sniper was aiming. Jacob fired. The bullet missed, but came close enough that the sniper flinched.

Not convinced about those 72 virgins, eh?

Jacob fired again, and the sniper's skull exploded.

The front edge of the container stack lay fifty yards away, and around that, the entrance to the conning tower where the bridge stood.

He had to get there before another of these crazies caught him in the open.

Jacob leapt to his feet, and immediately fell down again as his hip screamed in protest.

Gritting his teeth, he forced himself to ignore the pain and stand, using his free hand to support himself.

Nothing broken, or at least not so broken that his limbs wouldn't work. That furrow in his thigh from the bullet was bleeding a bit too much for his liking.

It didn't hurt nearly so much as his hip, though. He had landed on the side with his holster, and despite the roll he'd immediately tucked himself into, his whole weight had smashed against the steel weapon. He had probably fractured that hip.

A problem for another time, assuming he got to enjoy another time.

The container ship had left the Great Bitter Lake and entered the canal, headed north.

Headed toward the U.S. Navy ships that couldn't turn around.

Jacob hobbled toward the front of the ship. A terrorist rounded the corner, clutching an AK. He took the guy out with a single shot to the head. Getting to the corner, he peeked around, saw no one, and grabbed the guy's AK.

Just then, a burst of fire from an upper porthole forced him back around the corner.

Cursing, Jacob slung the AK and hobbled a few feet away to retrieve the sniper's rifle, a nice Dragunov, one of the more accurate Russian models. The Middle East was awash with them. He wondered how many civilians this weapon had killed.

He'd put it to better use. Hobbling back to the corner, cursing even louder now as the pain grew worse and the blood soaked his pants, he exposed his head and shoulders in a near-suicidal move, peering through the telescopic sight.

The guy in the porthole raised his AK.

Too late. Jacob took him out.

He struggled toward the door of the conning tower, caught a movement from his upper peripheral vision, and turned to see a figure at the top of the container stack. He snapped a shot in that direction, missing but forcing the guy to duck back out of sight.

He had to do the same with someone appearing at another porthole in the conning tower.

Then he was inside. The terrorists, confident of their numbers, hadn't closed and locked the door.

Tossing aside the rifle and unslinging the AK-47, he passed down a short corridor, ignoring a couple of closed doors until he found a staircase of steel mesh leading upwards.

He peeked up the stairwell, and saw a head move quickly out of sight.

Damn.

A shout in Arabic echoed down the hall. "Get the scientists to the bomb!"

He looked around, unsure of the source of the sound. He moved to a ground floor porthole and saw a fighter rush out of another door in the conning tower, leading three skinny young men.

Jacob wrenched open the porthole and fired. He took out the guard, then one scientist, then another.

The third scientist, hunched over and wrapping his arms around his head as if they could ward off a bullet, rounded the corner and disappeared.

Jacob hobbled for the door he had entered. If he caught up with that kid, he could find the bomb and defuse it.

A shadow darkened the threshold, resolving into two figures. Jacob paused. They were waiting for him. A clatter of several feet on the stairway told him they were coming that way too. He had to get out of there. He had to catch up to that last scientist.

Jacob reached for one of his grenades to toss through the doorway and take out those who stood between him and the bomb, only to find they had all tumbled out of his pocket in the fall.

His heart clenched. He was trapped.

CHAPTER TWENTY SEVEN

Jana zigzagged her way across the load of shipping containers, jumping the short spaces between them while keeping one eye on the Geiger counter and the other on her surroundings, convinced she'd get shot at any moment.

She could hear plenty of firing again up toward the front of the ship. She looked that way and could see no one. They must be on deck.

Beyond the ship, though, she saw something far more disturbing.

Coming the other direction along the narrow canal, hazy in the distant heat shimmer, was the gray silhouette of a warship.

Jana's heart sank. If she could see it, it was close enough to get annihilated by the bomb, and if there were nukes aboard like Jacob feared, they could very well go off in a chain reaction.

A crackling sound close by made her yelp. She looked around, frantic, but saw no enemies.

Jacob's voice called out, "Jana, you still alive?"

She gasped with relief. It was the radio on her belt.

Grabbing it, she spoke into it while continuing her zigzag search for any radiation signals. She couldn't afford to stop that for an instant.

"Where are you?" she asked.

"Trapped in the conning tower. They got me hemmed in. Look, Jana, they just sent a scientist out there to go to the bomb. Skinny guy with glasses. Looks totally different than the rest. I think he's going to go up one of the starboard ladders, one of the ones near the front. You've got to find him. I—"

Shots drowned out what he said next.

"Jacob? Jacob!"

"I'm still here. No way I'm getting out. Go find that guy. You're our only chance."

Cursing, she ran to the side of the container stack and peered over. At the front end, far from her, she saw a lone figure clambering up the ladder.

Jana lay down, aiming with her M16. She checked it was on single shot, then fired a round.

The guy didn't flinch.

She fired again. That got a reaction. She must have come closer this time. Still the man, visible only as a small silhouette against the glare from the sea, continued up the ladder.

Jana fired again, and again. Still he climbed.

I'm not good enough to hit him at this range.

Enraged with herself, she charged along the containers, hoping to get to the scientist's destination before he did.

She kept her eyes on the spot where she thought he'd come to the top of the ladder, hoping that he wasn't going to some hidden hatch on the side of the container stack.

Jana remained so focused she didn't notice another terrorist climbing up a ladder on the other side until he fired at her.

* * *

Aboard the *USS Brandywine*, Captain Cranston wasn't sure what to do. His radar technicians had observed a container ship moving toward them, soon confirmed by the forward spotters, and a moment later his radio officer had just patched him through to an urgent call from the Egyptian navy.

"*USS Brandywine*, this is Captain Mohammed Idris of the Canal Guards. One of our patrol boats was fired upon and sunk in the Great Bitter Lake. A container ship, the *Coral Atoll*, flying the Liberian flag, is moving your direction. Our shore sentries say the firing came from there when the patrol boat tried to stop them moving. It appears your agent's reports of a terrorist attack are true. We are sending more patrol boats and have contacted the Air Force, but we cannot get any more support to you for at least twenty minutes. We have a shore battery within range capable of sinking the ship, but we have not yet received permission from our superiors to fire upon the vessel."

"I understand, Captain Idris," Captain Cranston said, searching the canal ahead of him. To sink such a large ship would block the canal for months, leading to billions in lost revenue for this economically struggling nation. No one of Idris's rank could make that kind of decision on his own.

In the far distance, he could just make out the container vessel blocking their progress. The huge ship was at least a mile away, but if there was a nuke aboard, it wouldn't matter.

"Captain Idris, we have intelligence that this particular ship is under the control of a group called The Sword of the Righteous, and that it may be carrying a nuclear device. Do you have any intelligence to that effect?"

"A nuclear device! No, we have no such intelligence. And trust me, captain, in this situation I would tell you even if it meant revealing state secrets."

"I believe you, Captain Idris." The man sounded like a professional, someone who could think for himself.

"How firm is your intelligence?" the Egyptian asked. "This group is known to us, but has not yet many any great incursions into our country."

"Our intelligence is ... " *what do I tell him, that it's based on a wild story from a lone field agent who thinks they got uranium 235 from an archaeological site?* " ...not one hundred percent."

"But it is obviously terrorists on the boat. Even if they don't have the device you mention, they will try to ram you."

"We will not let that happen, Captain Idris."

"I understand, Captain Cranston. I will discuss the possibility of firing our shore battery at them with my staff. It is ... a difficult decision. We also have reports of a helicopter landing on the boat."

"That's an agent with the Central Intelligence Agency."

Captain Cranston had just revealed classified information to a member of a foreign military, something that could get him court marshaled, but damn the consequences. He had a whole fleet of men and women to protect.

"There's firing aboard," the Egyptian officer said.

"Then he's still alive. Good."

"Only one man?"

"Yes."

"One of our sentries was observing the ship with high-powered binoculars and said two people got out of the helicopter."

Captain Cranston blinked. "I don't know who the second person is."

What the hell is going on over there?

"It does not matter. Only two against a whole ship of trained fighters? Your men will not be able to survive for long."

"I'm afraid you might be right," Captain Cranston said, his jaw tightening.

"Captain, that ship may or may not have a nuclear device. I find it hard to believe that they do, but you are still in grave danger. They could ram you, or perhaps set off a large amount of conventional explosives. I—hold on." There was a pause as he spoke to someone in

133

Arabic. The radio signal cut off. A moment later it returned. "Captain Cranston. My superiors are still discussing the issue. I emphasized haste. They said they will give me an answer in a couple of minutes."

"We might not have a couple of minutes."

"I understand. And I wish you to know that if you feel compelled to fire in self-defense, that you have nothing to fear from us. In fact … " Captain Cranston could practically hear his counterpart's internal struggle, the constant fight between logic and orders that any military man knows so well. " … if you find yourself compelled to fire on the *Coral Atoll*, we will take appropriate action."

The way he said it, Captain Cranston knew what he meant. He'd order his shore batteries to fire on the container ship. Captain Idris couldn't express that out loud without endangering his command, but he wanted to tell the Naval officer what side he was on.

"Do you understand me, Captain Cranston?"

"I do. May I ask the nature of your shore batteries?"

"Harpoon Block II anti-ship cruise missiles."

Captain Cranston gave an approving nod. Those were the best available, produced by an American defense contractor and only available for sale with federal permission. Someone in Washington wanted the Suez Canal well defended.

"I'm glad to hear that, Captain Idris. In that case, I wish to inform you that I will fire on the *Coral Atoll*."

"Understood, Captain Cranston. May God have mercy on us."

"I certainly hope so. Over and out."

Because if we fire on the container ship, Agent Snow and whoever is with him will die.

He turned to his second in command. "Get the forward guns trained on that ship to fire on my command."

"Sir, why did the Egyptian captain not want to fire first?"

"The Egyptian military is full of rivalries and factions, and the lower officers are afraid of the generals who make up the junta running this country. If Idris tries to fire first, one of his fellow officers might try and remove him from command. But if we force his hand by firing first, he can order the shore batteries to fire and know that his command will be carried out. The damage will have already been done and they can blame the Americans."

To his credit, his second-in-command didn't mock the Egyptians. This was a rough area of the world, operating under very different rules. The officer simply turned to the dashboard and radioed down a message to gunnery control.

"Prepare forward guns, battery one of anti-ship missiles, and all three torpedo tubes, aimed at the container ship ahead of us. Prepare to fire on the captain's command."

Captain Cranston allowed himself a tight smile. Without his having to say so, his second-in-command had brought all available firepower to bear on the hostile ship.

Within moments, the armaments would be ready, and then Captain Arnold Cranston would have to make the most momentous decision of his career.

CHAPTER TWENTY EIGHT

Jana flinched as a bullet careened off the metal at her feet. She jerked her head around and saw a terrorist with an AK-47 standing just at the top of the front portside ladder. At the same moment, a thinner, younger Arab man wearing glasses poked his head over the top of the starboard side.

Making a split second decision, Jana fired at the scientist.

He disappeared, whether from getting hit or ducking out of the line of fire, Jana wasn't sure.

Another bullet whined past her head.

Jana went to one knee and aimed.

A third bullet went past her. Jana, amazed she was still alive, returned fire with her M16.

At the range they were at, the M16 was a much more accurate weapon in trained hands than an AK-47.

In trained hands. She wasn't trained. Not really. And this guy was.

Jana let off a round, missed, and let off another.

The guy went prone. She was pretty sure she hadn't hit him, and so she went prone too, cursing herself for not thinking of that first thing. Dad had drilled that into her head, but practicing in the woods with no one around was a whole different ballgame than trading fire with a real person.

"Ahmed, get your dirty ass up here!" the man shouted in Arabic.

"She'll shoot me," came a squawk from the other side of the ship.

So I haven't hit him, and it doesn't look like he'll make a showing until I'm dead.

She aimed, letting out a slow breath, focusing.

The terrorist let off another round, the bullet panging off the metal close by.

To her surprise, Jana barely flinched. She kept aiming, and squeezed the trigger.

And missed.

"Ahmed! Hurry up!"

The terrorist fired again, missing, before muttering something, ejecting his magazine, and reaching into a pouch slung over his shoulder to retrieve another magazine.

Out of ammo. He must have spent some firing at Jacob.

She aimed, and realized she wouldn't hit him. She'd fired several times already and missed every time. She simply wasn't good enough to be reliable at this range.

The only solution? Get closer.

Jana leapt to her feet, charging straight at the terrorist. He paused a second to gape, then got to one knee and pulled the magazine out of the pouch.

Someone was screaming. The scientist named Ahmed poked his head over the top and Jana fired a snapshot in his direction. She knew she wouldn't hit but hoped he'd duck back down. He didn't.

Jana ran pell-mell for the terrorist as he snapped the magazine into his Kalashnikov. She still heard screaming, but neither terrorist seemed to be making the sound.

Then she realized it was her screaming.

The terrorist leveled his AK-47.

Jana stopped, aimed for a stomach-churning moment, convinced he'd shoot first, and fired.

The terrorist took it full in the chest, falling back, arms flying wide. Jana swung around to fire at Ahmed, and saw him disappear into a hatch on top of one of the shipping containers.

Jana sprinted over and looked down just in time to see Ahmed leap off the bottom of a short ladder and disappear inside the shipping container. It was lit inside. Jana knew why.

Hoping Ahmed didn't have a gun, she held her own assault rifle in one hand as she clambered down the ladder, risking a fall every time she let go with her free hand to grasp the rung below. She only went down enough to swing around and aim at the scientists one-handed.

Ahmed stood at the opposite end of the shipping container by a large metal box. He pressed a timer, turned, and smiled.

For a moment, neither spoke, Jana too stunned to speak, and Ahmed looking at her with a smug expression on his face. At her hip, the Geiger counter let off a low, steady crackle.

"Turn off that timer or I'll shoot you where you stand." Jana's voice came out hoarse. She hated the tremor she heard in it.

"You speak our language? Then you must know that death holds no fear for me. My afterlife will be unimaginably better than my current existence."

Jana jumped off the ladder, falling the last few feet and landing with a clank on the metal floor. Ahmed did not move.

"Turn it off."

"You don't get to give me orders, Christian bitch."

Jana stalked forward, glancing at the timer. Nine minutes and forty-eight seconds.

"You'll kill thousands of fellow Muslims, maybe millions. Sunnis too."

"Those who are pure of heart will thank me as we share paradise. Those who are not, get what Allah has written for them."

"Idiot." She looked again at the time. She only saw a single button.

"It can be turned on," Ahmed said, chuckling, "but not off. I suppose you could fiddle with the wires. Do you know how to disarm a bomb? From the look on your face I'd say no."

Jana shuddered. She looked into the man's eyes in the dim light of the single, low-powered bulb hanging from the ceiling. All she saw there was madness.

Then those eyes widened.

She fired just as he leapt for her.

The force of the 5.56mm round at point blank range sent him flying back to bang against the wall. Ahmed fell to his knees, grinning.

Jana fired again, another round blasting through his chest.

His eyes rolled up, he whispered, "It is written," then fell face first onto the floor. He didn't move after that.

Jana turned and stared at the timer. Nine minutes and twenty-eight seconds. A mess of wires led from it into the metal casing.

Ahmed was right. She had no idea how to turn it off.

She ran for the ladder. She needed Jacob. If he wasn't alive, in less than ten minutes nobody within a mile radius would be.

CHAPTER TWENT NINE

Jacob was beginning to lose hope. He had taken cover in the doorway of a small side room in the middle of the hallway on the conning tower's ground floor. The AK-47 he'd taken off a dead terrorist was nearly out of ammo. On either end of the hallway, the guy's comrades kept popping out from their own doorways to fire at his position. Bullets whined and ricocheted up and down the hallway.

Jacob thought he might have two or three bullets left. If he charged, he'd be dead before he made it three steps. If he stayed here, these guys would eventually figure out why he wasn't firing back and charge as a group. He'd take out a couple, and then die.

And at any moment, that nuke might go off.

Every time he blinked, he was surprised that he got to open his eyes afterwards. Every time he took in a breath, the exhalation a moment later felt like a miracle.

It couldn't last. He needed to do something. Now.

He wasn't sure how long it had been since he had radioed Jana. She hadn't radioed back, and he'd been a bit too busy to chitchat. He could only assume she'd been killed or captured.

That brought up a sense of loss he didn't have time for. It was up to him now.

Taking a deep breath, he prepared to rush the staircase. He'd fire a shot at the outer door to keep those guys' heads down, and then rush for the stairs. When the terrorists there popped out to fire, he'd kill as many as he had bullets left for.

And after that? Well, it had been a good life.

Sort of. A useful one, anyway.

And at least he'd go down fighting.

Just as he summoned up the courage for a mad dash that would almost certainly end his life, he got surprised by a flurry of fire at the doorway entering the conning tower. He took a split-second peek and saw one of the terrorists lying dead, half in and half out of the door. He ducked his head back before anyone in the doorway leading to the stairwell could take a shot at him.

"You still there, Jacob?" Jana's voice called out.

His heart leapt. "Yeah!"

"You dropped your balls. Close your door. I'm going to get rid of one."

"My balls? Oh!"

Jacob slammed the metal ship's door. A second later it bashed into his shoulder as a shockwave burst down the corridor.

This woman has a hell of a way of speaking in code. Shows she's got her head together, though. These guys might understand English.

He flung open the door and rushed out, trying to ignore the ache in his hip as he limped along as fast as he could.

A terrorist staggered out of the stairwell, blood streaming from his body and yet still clutching an AK-47. Jacob took him out, ducked into the stairwell, and found the other two already dead. He grabbed a spare clip and snapped it into his weapon, then tucked a second clip in the back of his belt.

"Jacob!" he could hear Jana calling him through the ringing in his ears.

He turned to her. "Got a stun grenade?"

"Jacob, we—"

"Answer the question!"

"I don't know. What do they look like?" She pulled out two grenades, one a regular fragmentation kind, and the other with a light blue band painted around it signifying it was a stun grenade. He snatched both of them.

"We need to incapacitate the crew on deck and stop this ship."

"But Jacob—"

"Keep an eye on our rear."

He clambered up the steps, pain lancing through his body with every step. There were two stories above him. The deck would be on the top one.

Jacob didn't have time to check every corner or clear every side room or passage. He needed to get up there yesterday.

Which is why he almost missed the guy lurking around the corner of the stairwell on the first floor.

The terrorist swung around on him, firing a pistol as he went. Jacob just had enough time to dodge, feeling the hot pain of a graze along his ribs before caving the guy's face in with the butt of his assault rifle.

Fire down below. Jana was trading shots down the stairwell with someone who had tried to sneak up on them.

Jacob kept going.

At the top floor, he found the door to the bridge closed and no doubt locked. He had expected this. Yanking off his belt, he used it to lash the fragmentation grenade to the lock, pulled the pin, and hobbled around the corner. Jana was still one floor down and hopefully out of the blast zone. He shouted a warning but didn't have time to check if she heard.

The explosion flung the door open, and before the terrorists inside could react Jacob tossed the stun grenade in there.

A flash and a bang, and Jacob barreled in, firing as he went. All the terrorists were down and stunned, incapacitated for the next several minutes. He shot them anyway.

Then he looked out the front of the deck and his heart sunk.

He could clearly see an American cruiser in the distance, its forward guns lowering to aim at him.

Jacob yanked the throttle to stop, then full reverse. He knew it wouldn't be enough. A ship this massive had so much momentum it took ages to slow down. He needed to do more.

Jacob grabbed the radio to call out, only to find a sliver of metal from the door lock neatly embedded in the transceiver.

"Oh, crap."

He hauled on the ship's wheel and steered the ship toward the edge of the canal. After a moment, the ship lurched. The starboard side ground against the side of the canal with a terrible scraping and groaning sound.

Jana rushed into the room.

"I found the nuke!"

"Why didn't you tell me?"

"You didn't give me a chance."

"Did you disarm it?"

"I don't know how. One of them started a ten-minute timer. That was probably five minutes ago."

Jacob gave one last terrified look at his own Navy, which was obviously about to blow them out of the water, and hobbled for the door.

"Show me."

Five minutes? He didn't have time to get there and figure out how to disable the thing.

And he probably wouldn't get there anyway, because a Navy cruiser could turn this entire container ship into a kill zone within a few seconds.

* * *

"Ready to fire, captain," Captain Cranston's second-in-command reported.

Captain Cranston studied the *Coral Atoll* through a pair of powerful binoculars.

The ship had veered to one side, and was now grinding against the canal bank, ploughing up soil and slowing down. The work of that Agent Snow? It must be.

He got on the radio.

"Captain Idris, are you still there?"

"Yes. Do you see that the pilot of the *Coral Atoll* is trying to beach the ship?"

"I do. That must be the work of our agent."

"We have sentries close to its position, and they report heavy firing and explosions until a couple of minutes ago. Now it is silent. Perhaps your man has taken control?"

"Perhaps."

"Are you going to fire on the ship?"

"I ... haven't decided."

"Captain Cranston. If there is a nuclear device on board, firing on the ship might disable it."

"And spread radioactive material all over your canal, as well as leave a ship blocking it for months to come."

"A terrible outcome instead of a disastrous one," the Egyptian pointed out. "I still have received no definitive orders from the generals."

The frustration in the officer's words were palpable.

"The ship will stop before it reaches us," Captain Cranston said. "I've ordered all our ships to stop too."

"You are well in range of even the smallest nuclear device," Captain Idris said. "If any terrorists remain on board, they will try to set it off. I suggest you fire. Once you do, I will ... be free to act as well. The safest option is to hit the *Coral Atoll* with overwhelming firepower and hope to destroy the device, keeping it from going off."

Captain Cranston gritted his teeth. What the Egyptian said made sense, but what if Agent Snow had really taken control of the ship? He'd be killing a fellow American.

The fact that the CIA man would understand and approve of his action, would do the same in his place, didn't make it any easier.

"Captain Cranston?" the Egyptian officer asked.

"Let's hold for a moment. If you hear any more firing, tell me immediately. That will indicate that our man doesn't have full control of the vessel. If there's any more firing, I'll give the order to open fire."

And may God have mercy on my soul.

CHAPTER THIRTY

Jacob Snow groaned as he forced himself up the ladder as fast as he could. His injured hip barely responded, and the heat and stress of the fight had begun to make his head swim.

An instinct for survival urged him on. Even more than that, an instinct to get the job done.

After Afghanistan, he had never really thought of his life as his own. Instead, it was in pawn to Aaron Peters, the dead father of that remarkable woman climbing the ladder just below him, and that debt could never be repaid. His life, his very soul, would always be in hock.

And that drove him to do this sort of stuff.

He hauled himself onto the top of the shipping container stack, his hip twinging in protest, his thigh and side leaking blood.

Didn't even check to see if the area was clear. I'm slipping.

It was clear, though. No terrorists in sight. None alive, anyway. He spotted the hatch not far off and hobbled for it, sparing a nervous glance at the warship a mile away. It still hadn't fired. Surprising.

"Never complain about good luck in the field. There's a severe shortage of it." That's what Aaron Peters always used to say.

Jacob didn't bother with the ladder leading into the shipping container. He grabbed the lip of the hatch and dropped down.

The pain that shot through his hip nearly knocked him out. The sight of a nuclear bomb a few steps away kept him awake.

He struggled to his feet, only managing a crawl across the shipping container to the device.

The timer said ten seconds.

Grasping the bomb casing, he hauled himself to his feet. Jana thumped to the floor behind him, dropping down just like he did, eager to get to ground zero.

Nine seconds.

The casing was sealed shut. He could see several heavy screws holding a front panel in place. No way he'd open that in time.

Eight seconds.

Several wires ran from the timer into the casing. Only one was needed, so the others must be decoys, primed to blow the bomb if they were pulled.

Seven seconds.

The timer casing was cheap plastic, two halves held together with tiny screws.

Six seconds.

"Knife," he said, holding his hand out like some surgeon.

"I don't have one."

Five seconds.

"Hair pin. Nail file. Anything!"

Jana bent down and rummaged through the pockets of the dead scientist against the nearby wall.

Four seconds. Three seconds.

Pull a wire at random and hope for the best.

Jana handed him a thin metal screwdriver of the kind people used for fixing eyeglasses. It was just the right size for the screws holding the timer together.

He didn't have time to unscrew them, though. Instead, he jammed the tip between the two plastic halves and twisted. The back popped off.

Two seconds.

He found the wire leading from the timer to the casing and yanked it out of the circuitry.

One second.

The timer held at one second.

"We did it," Jacob whispered.

For a second they both stared at the timer.

"We did it," Jacob said again.

Jana replied by throwing up on the floor.

Jacob burst out laughing, the tension of the last few days, and especially the last few minutes, bursting forth in a flood of relief.

"Sorry," he manage to choke out. "I'm not laughing at you."

Actually he was a bit, and at himself. He had puked after his first combat.

Jana didn't seem to take it the wrong way. She was actually laughing too as strings of drool oozed down from a green grin.

Still chuckling, Jacob helped her to her feet. Jana wiped her mouth with her shirt, then unbuttoned it and tossed it aside, leaving only her halter top.

"I should have been a gentleman and given you my shirt," Jacob said.

"It's too bloody."

For some reason that set off another round of laughter in both of them. The red number one on the timer glared at them like the middle finger of a thwarted devil.

He put a hand on her shoulder. "I have to admit I had my doubts, but you turned out to be a good sidekick."

"You got that wrong. You're my sidekick," she replied with a smile.

"Well, you saved your sidekick's ass several times on this mission. OK, boss. Let's get out of here."

Jana glanced at the bomb. "You sure that thing is secure?"

"Yeah. We can let the local bomb disposal crew handle it from here. The Egyptians have plenty of experience with that. Not with nukes, but the principal is the same. Let's get to the chopper and radio in."

Now that it was all over, weariness hung on Jacob like a suit of lead. The ladder felt like it was a thousand feet tall, and climbing every rung took more effort than climbing Mt. Everest. At the top, he couldn't even stand, only roll out of the way to give Jana room to come up.

And that saved his life.

A shot rang out, the bullet skimming through the air just above Jacob as he lay on top of the shipping container.

A terrorist knelt at the other side of the container stack, aiming an AK-47 at him. A bit beyond him, a second was just climbing up to the top of the ladder.

Jacob rolled onto his front as more bullets chased him, and opened up with a three-round burst, taking out the man firing at him. A second burst took out the other one just as he clambered off the ladder.

Jacob searched around. He saw no more left to kill.

That must have been the last. I'll check, but I think it's all over now.

* * *

"Captain Cranston, our sentries have reported more firing on the *Coral Atoll*."

Captain Idris's message came through just as the Naval officer was beginning to feel some hope.

The Naval captain's fist clenched. *Here we go.* "Thank you, Captain Idris. I'll give the order to fire."

"And I'll give my orders right after you do."

146

The second-in-command reached for the intercom to the gunnery officer, but Cranston grabbed it first. He was the captain and, unfortunately, it was his ultimate responsibility. He would give the command personally.

"Forward guns fire, followed by the torpedoes and missiles."

He had already ordered the guns and missiles to aim for the container stack, and the torpedoes to hit the waterline. His hope was that the surface hits would kill any terrorists and perhaps disable the bomb, while the torpedoes would sink the ship, keeping any remaining members of The Sword of the Righteous from getting to the bomb.

The shore battery would probably pummel any survivors of the *USS Brandywine's* initial volley, but it was best to make sure.

That ship had to be hit so hard that not even a cockroach would be left alive.

* * *

Only by chance did Jacob see the plume from the cruiser's guns firing. He had just glanced over at the ship while he stumbled for the helicopter as fast as his battered body would allow.

The fire from the American cruiser proved to him that he could actually run a bit faster. Jana came right beside him.

"Incoming!" Jacob shouted.

Jana hit the deck. Jacob didn't, because if he didn't get to the chopper, he'd be dead in a few seconds.

Or sooner.

The shot hit the front of the container stack, making the entire ship shake. The container just above the explosion got lifted in the air and then fell, hitting the conning tower with an ear-splitting clang.

Jacob kept running. A second shot hit a moment later, blasting the deck of the conning tower. Jacob stumbled, regained his footing, and made it to the chopper, which still sat in a pool of its own fuel. The fumes made Jacob even more lightheaded than he already was.

That satellite phone had better still be working.

He hoped a stray bullet hadn't taken it out. He grabbed it.

"Wallace, you still there?"

"Who is this? Identify yourself," a strange voice answered in English.

"This is Agent Snow of the CIA, aboard the grounded container ship. Is this the *USS Brandywine*?" he asked, wondering and hoping if he was still patched into the ship.

"This is the *USS Brandywine*."

"Cease fire immediately! The bomb has been defused. Patch me through to Captain Cranston."

He realized he was talking to the radio officer, a complete stranger who probably didn't know the extent of the threat Jacob had explained earlier to the captain.

There was a pause. Jacob tried to anticipate the radio officer's thinking. Would he listen to a strange voice coming over the line? Would he realize that Jacob would have to be the person he said he was in order to have a private channel to the ship?

Jana crawled toward him, hugging the top of the shipping container, obviously afraid of more shots from the *Brandywine's* bow guns.

But what Jacob could see made him a lot more afraid than a few artillery shells.

The flare of missiles being launched from the ship, and the white lines of three torpedoes churning through the water straight at them.

"Captain Cranston here. Is this Agent Snow?"

Jacob could have sobbed with relief. "Yes! The bomb has been defused. The ship is cleared."

"You sure, agent?"

"Yes!"

The missiles hurtled at them, followed by the torpedoes like a trio of steel sharks.

The wire-guided torpedoes took a hard right, exploding on the bank a couple of hundred yards away. The missiles veered at the last moment, streaking over the container ship and flying beyond for a quarter of a mile before hitting the water, sending up plumes almost as tall as the container ship itself.

Jacob gasped with relief.

"Look!" Jana screamed.

The trails of half a dozen missiles arced over the desert to their east, headed right for them.

Oh God, the Egyptians fired too.

Jacob glanced at Jana, their eyes locking.

At least she died a hero, like her dad.

His ears filled with the roar of the incoming missiles, but then they, too, passed overhead, slamming into the desert a mile beyond the canal.

An unfamiliar voice came over the line, speaking English with an Egyptian accent.

"How do you say that in English, Captain Cranston. A 'close call?'"

"Yes, Captain Idris," the Naval officer said, laughing. "I'd definitely say that was a close call."

CHAPTER THIRTY ONE

A field near Asilah, northwestern Morocco
Two weeks later ...

Jana looked out over the excavation. The crew had done well in her absence, and even better in the few days since she had returned. The layers of soil had been stripped down to the Roman villa, and now the crew was carefully uncovering that important find, revealing a breathtaking mosaic decorated with the signs of the zodiac, just as she had predicted.

The rest of the villa was equally impressive, and lucky crewmembers had turned up fine pottery, a bowl that would be pieced back together in the lab, and even a lone gold earring.

The field report would make good reading. For the general public, she was already writing an article in Arabic for *Al Alam*, one of Morocco's biggest daily newspapers, and had done an interview for national television.

Brian, the older graduate student she had built up a rapport with, strolled over, canteen in hand.

"Want a drink?"

She took a long pull from the canteen. The sun felt hotter today, but considering what she'd been through, she barely noticed.

"After that Roman earring you found, we should be celebrating with champagne," Jana said.

He treated her to a warm smile. "I could probably arrange that. Glad you made it back in time for me to find it. Is your sister feeling better?"

"Oh, yes, she's fine now."

Jana had invented a sick sister needing an emergency operation to explain her sudden disappearance. Everyone had, of course, accepted that without question. The lie had made her feel distant from her crew, however, and the fact that she could never tell the truth made that distance permanent.

The only person she could talk about it with was Jacob Snow. They had said their goodbyes in Cairo, four days after the events at the Suez Canal and after a long debriefing with the Egyptian intelligence agency and the local CIA office. To the news media, there was a simple hijacking on the canal intercepted by Egyptian forces. No mention that the *USS Brandywine* and her escort ships were even in the area.

It turned out they didn't have to be. The hardliners in Iran had backed down, returning the American hostages. The imams had declared an interim government for the sake of national stability, installing a compromise candidate as interim president. For the moment, the reformists and Islamists in Iran had been forced into an uneasy truce.

It wasn't the end of the story, she knew, but whatever other espionage took place because of that mess, that was Jacob's department, not hers. She wouldn't ask and he wouldn't tell.

Still, she had his number in Greece.

"It works when I'm not on assignment. Call if you want to talk about your dad, or maybe you can show me some ancient ruins or something if you're in the neighborhood."

That had been said with an awkward smile Jana couldn't quite read.

She might do that. She still had a lot of questions about her father, questions she wasn't sure he had permission to answer. Questions she wasn't even sure she wanted answered.

But it would be interesting to see what kind of man Jacob Snow was when he wasn't getting shot at.

"Thinking of her?" Brian asked.

"Hm?" she said, snapping out of her reverie.

"Your sister."

"Oh. Right. My sister. Yeah. She's recovering. Getting some much-needed rest. Well, let's get some more work done. We only have a couple of good hours of daylight left."

She headed to the nearest excavation square, trying to focus on her work, and yet the thought of her father's protégé in Greece would follow her for the rest of the day.

And the day after that.

* * *

The Greek Cycladic Islands, that same evening ...

Gabriella executed a perfect dive from the deck of Jacob's sailing boat, slipping into the brilliantly clear Mediterranean water with barely a ripple. Jacob lounged on deck, watching the younger woman as she did a backstroke, their eyes locked on each other.

"Aren't you going to come in?" Gabriella called to him.

"In a minute. In the meantime, how about you dive again?"

Gabriella laughed, flipped over, and did a breaststroke back to him.

"That's the fifth time you asked that."

"Sixth. There's nothing quite as beautiful as a young woman diving. That new bikini certainly helps."

"I thought you'd like it. All right. I'll dive again," Gabriella said, climbing back onto the ship as the water ran off her olive skin. "But after that you swim too. Do your cuts still sting in salt water?"

"No. They're fine now."

Jacob had made up a story about getting caught in a riot in Liberia to explain his injuries. The various scrapes and bruises had mostly healed by the time he'd returned to Athens, but there was no hiding the two graze wounds or the hairline fracture on his hip that had left him with a deep bruise the size of a dinner plate.

He felt bad about having to lie, and wished that he could tell her even a little bit of the real story.

Gabriella smiled down at him, her curly black hair dripping, her body framed by the setting sun.

"All right, I'll do another dive. And then we'll cook up those fish I caught. And after that, I'm going to torture you until you give up that job of yours and settle down in Rome."

That last bit took Jacob by surprise. While Gabriella had frequently urged him to give up his supposed job as an organizer of international aid to warzones—this wasn't the first time he'd come home beat up— she had never suggested settling in her hometown before.

"Are you getting serious on me?" Jacob asked, one eyebrow going up.

"Why not?" she bent down and jabbed a finger in Jacob's chest. "I'm getting sick of the clubbing scene, and something more stable would sure do you some good. I've never understood why you keep at that job."

And you never will, Jacob thought with despair, *because I can't explain it to you.*

No civilian could understand.

Well, there was one civilian, way over in Morocco on an archaeological dig.

He wondered if she'd call him. He wondered what she had thought about his half-serious offer of a trip to the archaeological sites of Greece.

Most of all, he wondered if he would ever see her again.

His gut told him he would. Jacob couldn't say how or when, but he had the feeling their paths would cross again.

"Watch!"

Gabriella shot him a grin over her shoulder, then tucked into an expert dive into the water.

Jacob watched, thinking of someone else.

Then his gaze strayed across the water to an island about three kilometers away. The side facing them was a jagged cliff, the water splashing on the rocks at its base, the top covered in bushes.

A good vantage point. In Afghanistan there'd be a sniper up there.

His focused zeroed in on the clifftop.

If I was going to position myself, it would be right about there, where that olive tree gives a bit of extra shade and the top of the cliff makes a bit of a hollow.

A warm kiss on the lips distracted him. He hadn't even heard her get out of the water.

"Stop working," Gabriella said before kissing him again.

Jacob wrapped his arms around her sleek form. "Do I look like I'm working to you?"

"You get that distant look, like you're a million miles away." Gabriella looked troubled. He knew he wasn't being fair, not giving this wonderful woman the attention she deserved.

"You're right. No more work today."

They kissed again, and for a moment Jacob forgot about the troubles of the world.

* * *

A perfect shot.

The sniper watched Jacob and his girlfriend kiss on the boat from his vantage point some three kilometers away. He lay in a prone position atop a rocky cliff, hidden from view by a cluster of bushes, a natural depression in the clifftop, and the shade of an olive tree. The breeze was mild for this time of day, and at this range he could be sure of a hit.

Yes, the range was only 500 meters short of the world record, but he'd made shots like this before, and in a lot worse conditions too.

Oh, God, it's tempting.

The sniper's finger was tight on the trigger of his McMillan TAC-50, one of the best sniper's rifles in the business. He could make this shot, put an end to it all right now.

153

Yeah, it was tempting.

Or maybe take out the girl. Torture him a bit, like Jacob Snow had tortured him so much.

But no. That would only warn him.

And he didn't really want to shoot him with a long-range shot anyway.

He wanted to savor the look in Jacob's eyes as he explained why he was going to die, as Jacob finally had to confront the consequences to his actions.

Besides, he couldn't. Not yet. He needed information from him first.

Job first. You need him to lead you where you need to go.

The sniper gritted his teeth.

Damn it! Why is it that the people we hate the most are the ones we always depend on?

He had to wait. To follow. To learn.

Then to kill.

Slowly, with infinite reluctance, the sniper took his finger off the trigger.

"This isn't forgiveness, Jacob Snow," he whispered. "This is a stay of execution."

NOW AVAILABLE!

TARGET TWO
(The Spy Game—Book #2)

"Thriller writing at its best... A gripping story that's hard to put down."
--Midwest Book Review, Diane Donovan (re Any Means Necessary)

"One of the best thrillers I have read this year. The plot is intelligent and will keep you hooked from the beginning. The author did a superb job creating a set of characters who are fully developed and very much enjoyable. I can hardly wait for the sequel."
--Books and Movie Reviews, Roberto Mattos (re Any Means Necessary)

From #1 bestselling and USA Today bestselling author Jack Mars, author of the critically acclaimed *Luke Stone* and *Agent Zero* series (with over 5,000 five-star reviews), comes an explosive new action-packed espionage series that takes readers on a wild ride across Europe, America, and the world.

Jacob Snow—elite soldier-turned-CIA agent, haunted by his tortured past—is one of the CIA's greatest assets. When a terrorist group sets its eyes on the greatest archeological treasure of the holiest city, Jacob, dispatched, knows he has little time to reach Jerusalem before it sparks an international war.

Jacob knows, even more, that he cannot solve the case without partnering with the mysterious archeologist he hopes to *not* fall in love with.

As they spring into action to decode the ancient riddles and stop them, they soon realize the plot goes deeper than they could have imagined. With the fate of the world in the balance, they may just be out of time.

An unputdownable action thriller with heart-pounding suspense and unforeseen twists, TARGET TWO is the debut novel in an exhilarating new series by a #1 bestselling author that will make you fall in love with a brand-new action hero—and keep you turning pages late into the night. Perfect for fans of Dan Brown, Daniel Silva and Jack Carr.

Book #3 in the series—TARGET THREE—is now also available.

Jack Mars

Jack Mars is the USA Today bestselling author of the LUKE STONE thriller series, which includes seven books. He is also the author of the new FORGING OF LUKE STONE prequel series, comprising six books; of the AGENT ZERO spy thriller series, comprising twelve books; of the TROY STARK thriller series, comprising three books; and of the SPY GAME thriller series, comprising three books.

Jack loves to hear from you, so please feel free to visit www.Jackmarsauthor.com to join the email list, receive a free book, receive free giveaways, connect on Facebook and Twitter, and stay in touch!

BOOKS BY JACK MARS

THE SPY GAME
TARGET ONE (Book #1)
TARGET TWO (Book #2)
TARGET THREE (Book #3)

TROY STARK THRILLER SERIES
ROGUE FORCE (Book #1)
ROGUE COMMAND (Book #2)
ROGUE TARGET (Book #3)

LUKE STONE THRILLER SERIES
ANY MEANS NECESSARY (Book #1)
OATH OF OFFICE (Book #2)
SITUATION ROOM (Book #3)
OPPOSE ANY FOE (Book #4)
PRESIDENT ELECT (Book #5)
OUR SACRED HONOR (Book #6)
HOUSE DIVIDED (Book #7)

FORGING OF LUKE STONE PREQUEL SERIES
PRIMARY TARGET (Book #1)
PRIMARY COMMAND (Book #2)
PRIMARY THREAT (Book #3)
PRIMARY GLORY (Book #4)
PRIMARY VALOR (Book #5)
PRIMARY DUTY (Book #6)

AN AGENT ZERO SPY THRILLER SERIES
AGENT ZERO (Book #1)
TARGET ZERO (Book #2)
HUNTING ZERO (Book #3)
TRAPPING ZERO (Book #4)
FILE ZERO (Book #5)
RECALL ZERO (Book #6)
ASSASSIN ZERO (Book #7)
DECOY ZERO (Book #8)

Printed in Great Britain
by Amazon